The Hut

The Hut

By Dr. H

© 2022 by Dr. H. (Harry Hueston)

All rights reserved.

This book or any portion thereof may not be reproduced or used in any manner whatsoever without the express written permission of the publisher except for the use of brief quotations in a book review.

ISBN: 979-8-9857183-0-0

Acknowledgements:

This book is a work of fiction. The characters and events are a creation of the author. Certain locations mentioned in this book exist. Their names and locations are the results of several discussions with the author's in-laws who have resided in Key Marathon for the past fifty years.

The author would like to thank the Good Lord for assisting me in the creation of this novel. He also would like to thank his wife of fifty years who assisted in the writing and editing of this novel. In addition, he would like to thank the Hill families, who contributed to identifying various locations in Marathon and who assisted in the editing of this book, the Malone family whose son created the hydrodynamics theory on the impacts of hurricanes in the Florida Keys, and the Pelican family, my daughter who assisted in the various Spanish translations, and whose daughter helped design the cover of this book. Finally, the author would like to thank the homicide squad in the Amarillo Police Department and their Captain, Erick Bohannon who have guided me through the intricacies of crime scene in the sand.

May God Bless all the readers of this book. Thanks Harry

Chapter One: The Hut

August 18, 2021

The phone rang at 3:50 p.m. It was my Uncle Harry. As a retired chief of police and a criminal justice professor, he knew a lot about police work. He and his wife, Aunt Mimi, were down in the Florida Keys visiting my family during the tickling season.

"Katie, please get over here ASAP. I think I found a body buried along the seawall here at the Hut."

"Crud," I muttered. My name is Katie Hood. I am a homicide detective working in the Mangrove County Sheriff's Department.

"Dad," I called. "Please head onto the beach at the Hut. Uncle Harry needs me now."

He immediately started the boat.

When I arrived at the Hut, people were everywhere,

pushing closer and closer, while Uncle Harry tried to keep them away from the suspected homicide scene. I jumped on to the shoreline of the Hut and saw he'd blocked off a semicircle about twenty-five feet wide to keep everyone away.

I ran over to him and an awful stench hit me. "That is a decaying body," I told him.

"Right, I know," my uncle grumbled, "that's why I called you here."

The stench coming into this area was unbearable, and the people were still clamoring to see what was happening. I immediately contacted headquarters to get a few patrol units here ASAP. My uncle and I began to create a crib to place around the suspected crime scene. A crib is an investigative tool when a homicide scene is in the sand. It's used to keep the sand from sliding back into the dugout hole of a possible crime scene. While trying to protect the scene, I had to get another lounge chair to make a sieve for the sand once we began digging around the location of the body.

We made the crib from two long lounge chairs and two folding chairs. There was one additional lounge chair we used as a sieve to see if there was any evidence left in the sand. Once the crib was made, we got two shovels from the Hut's maintenance man, Sam. We couldn't wait on the arrival of the police, who were twenty minutes away. It was time to begin our investigation, which was all right, given our credentials. My uncle was a retired chief of police with thirty years of service in two different states and a former Army officer in the Military Police Corps. I had thirteen years in law enforcement under my belt and was currently working as a homicide detective in the local sheriff's department.

Slowly, we took shovelfuls of sand and carefully placed them on the makeshift sieve. We had dug down only a few inches when Uncle Harry said, "Stop, I have something here."

We brushed sand away from the object and saw the outline of a leg. Then, as we carefully cleared more sand away from the leg, we uncovered a body. It was wrapped in a plastic tarp and was nude, with no tattoos, marks, or any other identifying characteristics.

"Crud, I muttered for the second time, "this is going to be a long day."

Two Hours Earlier
I was enjoying my first day off in weeks. As I said before, my name is Katie Hood. I'm thirty-five years old and single. I have been working in law enforcement since I was twenty-one. I am a detective in the homicide section at the Mangrove County Sheriff's Department. I live in Point Key, an island adjacent to Key Marathon. The Hut is a popular gathering place at the beach in Point Key with a pool, bar, restaurant, and a great view of the water. I'd been to the Hut a thousand times over the past decade and today was another day I would be enjoying a meal there. Today would be my first time lobster

diving all year. I wanted to get an early start.

My day started at 10:00 a.m. with my diving for lobsters in the Bay (called the Gulf of Mexico). Lobster season starts for snorkelers on August 6, and on that day, I'd been finishing up a homicide investigation in Marathon Key. So I was thrilled to finally have some precious time off.

Lobster season is called the tickling season here in the Keys. The phrase "tickling the lobsters" is used to describe how a diver uses a tickle stick that tickles the lobster's antenna, making them shoot backward into a bait net. The start of the tickling season is crazy; people are everywhere and everything is packed, including the Hut.

My day started when myDad, and my two brothers, Ryan and Mike, anchored our boat in the Bay and tried to locate some lobsters. Unfortunately, the water in the Bay was muddy and filled with sea grass. It was not an ideal situation. After forty minutes of diving, we didn't find a single lobster. Dad suggested we leave the area and head for the ocean. I suggested we go to the Rockpile, a site known only to the locals that was likely to have lobsters. We arrived at the site, dropped anchor, and I dove in. The ocean was clear, blue, and very warm. I was down about twenty feet when I saw the antennas of lobsters. I took my tickle stick, dove down another ten feet, and caught two lobsters in seconds.

I got to the surface and yelled to everyone, "Lobsters are here!"

Within seconds, my brothers were in the water, diving

down and getting their own. I dove down one more time and caught another big one. Suddenly, something shining at the bottom of the ocean floor caught my eye. I went closer, moved some rocks, and found a coin. I put the coin in the waistband of my swimsuit and headed for the surface. I got to the surface and swam to the boat. Once in the boat, I showed the coin to Dad.

"Where did you find this?" he asked.

"Out there about twenty-five feet south of the Rockpile," I panted, trying to catching my breath. "Can you take me there?" he asked.

"Sure, let's go," I replied.

We jumped back into the water and dove down. I wasn't sure exactly where I found the coin, but soon recognized the location and swam over. I pointed the tickle stick at Dad and then signaled that I had to leave because I was out of breath. I headed up; Dad stayed down. While he was there, he saw another coin in the same area, then another. He put these inside his swimsuit and swam up to the surface.

"Ryan, please throw the bait net and the snapper net to Katie," yelled Dad.

"OK, Dad," Ryan stated.

I grabbed the nets and swam over to Dad. "Here, take these two coins and put them into the bait net, then stay here I am going down one more time." He dove down, then he came back, holding a small wooden box.

"What's that?" I asked,

"I don't know yet, let's get it into the boat and check it out," Dad said.

We got to the boat, climbed the ladder, put the box in the boat, and then looked at the coins.

"Dang," I exclaimed. "These look like old gold coins."

"Pirate treasure," shouted Ryan, "We're going to be rich!"

"Shut up," I told him, "Be quiet, and look at these things for a moment."

We opened the box and found more coins inside. That's when I got the call from Uncle Harry. We took off immediately and drove the boat onto the shore at the Hut.

Chapter Two: The Scene

August 18, 2021

At 4:30 p.m., Homicide Sergeant Detective Doaks arrived at the scene.

"Detective Hood, what did you screw up now?'" he asked.

I did not like Doaks. He was a thirty-year veteran police officer who was twice divorced, overweight, and did not believe in the use of forensics in any murder investigation.

"Hello, Sgt. Doaks," I replied. Doaks was a real pain in my hind parts, but he was the lead homicide detective, and I reported to him.

"Give me what you have so far," he said.

"We just uncovered a body buried in the sand about five minutes ago. We're waiting for the medical examiner to get here," I explained.

"Did you find anything on the body, scars, marks, tats?"

he asked.

"Nothing on the body, nothing found in the evidence from the sand, and no witnesses yet."

Doaks then turned and looked at my uncle. "Who the h - - l are you? What the h - - l are

you doing in my crime scene?" he demanded.

"Cool it, Doaks," I said with a roll of my eyes, "This is my uncle. He's a retired police chief who has just as many years of investigating homicides as you, so please introduce yourself to him and try to be civil."

Doaks backed off a little and stuck out his hand. My uncle was cool about it. He shook his hand and said nothing. Thankfully, no further explanation was needed.

Doaks took over the crime scene. He directed the two responding officers, Morgan and Juanito, to start taking witness statements from the thirty or so onlookers from the pool and the beach. When the officers left, the Doaks took a chair and sat down, looking tired.

"What are you doing sitting in the crime scene? Get your hind parts up now." I said as I pushed a strand of sandy hair off my face.

"Shut up, Hood, I am not feeling well, and the chair is *not* close to the scene. Besides, I need to use the restroom. Where is it?" Doaks whined.

Just another day working with Sergeant Detective Doaks, I thought.

When Doaks left, I directed the crime scene investigators

to begin photographing the crime scene. Hundreds of pictures were taken, and the scene was documented. I borrowed a laptop from the responding officer's vehicle, and began to document the day's events. My attention was directed toward the body once Dr. Spock, the Mangrove County medical examiner, arrived. Dr. Spock believed in using all forms of forensics to assist in his examination of a dead body.

"Detective Hood, was any evidence found at the crime scene or around the body?" he asked.

"No" I replied, "we have nothing yet."

Spock directed me and the two responding officers to assist him in pulling the body out of the ground. We hauled it into a body bag and then put the bag onto the gurney.

"Keep that plastic tarp around the body; we may find more evidence once I get it back to the morgue," Dr. Spock said, sounding optimistic. "Detective Hood, can you join me at the autopsy tomorrow around 8:00 a.m.? I am stacked up with dead bodies, and this homicide has to processed immediately."

"OK," I stated, "but what about Detective Doaks?"

"Where the heck is Doaks?" asked Dr. Spock. "I didn't see him on scene."

"He is in the restroom," I replied. "Do you want him there too?"

"Yes, if he thinks he can hold it long enough. He can't leave in the middle of my autopsy exam," Spock said impatiently.

Doaks returned to the scene fifteen minutes later. "Where is the medical examiner?" he asked.

"He was here. He removed the body from the scene and left," I informed him.

"Well crap, why did he leave so soon?" Doaks asked.

"Because you were gone for the past forty-five minutes. Now can we get this scene processed?" I asked, rolling my eyes.

"Oh, kiss off, Hood. What have you done so far?" Doaks asked.

I explained what we had done so far and then suggested getting a cadaver dog and some ground penetrating radar to make sure there were no other bodies buried here.

"Are you nuts?" Doaks exclaimed. "Why do we need cadaver dogs or ground radar?"

"Because I want to make sure that there are no other bodies buried here, since we already have one," I stated.

Now Doaks was really pissed. "Come over here, Hood," he ordered.

He took me away from the crime scene and then chewed me out. "What a waste of resources. Dogs! Ground penetrating radar! You and your forensics crap are a huge waste of time!" he said angrily. "Now get back to the crime scene, finish our measurements and statements, and then meet me at headquarters ASAP. Got it?"

"Doaks, just wait a second," I pleaded. "We need to be thorough with this homicide and cover all our bases. Think about your reputation as a good homicide detective in our department and in the Keys. I want this investigation to be complete, and these two tools can do that!"

"OK," Doaks said reluctantly, "but I want your report on my desk by 8:00 a.m. tomorrow, got it, Hood?"

"Yes, sir," I replied happily.

Now it was 11:00 p.m. I was hungry and still wearing my swimsuit.

Great, I thought, *where can I get a cadaver dog and some ground penetrating radar equipment at this hour?*

Chapter Three: Clutch

August 18, 2021

Charles Thomas Hudson, known to everyone as Clutch, was the supplier of any unique homicide tools cops needed in the Keys. He graduated from the Florida Department of Public Safety Academy with me in 2012 and was now working for the Florida Bureau of Investigation.

He earned his nickname due to his unique ability to locate many forms of specialized police equipment used in homicide investigations.

At 11:15 p.m., I called his cell.

"What?" Clutch muttered.

"Hi, Clutch, it's Hood. Did I disturb you?" I asked.

"Naw, I was catching up on my forensics updates. What do you need now, Hood?" he asked.

"Cadaver dogs and a ground penetrating radar unit," I

quickly said.

"Are you nuts?" Clutch yelled. "These items are already in use and are booked months in advance. Where am I going to find one of these things now?"

"Come on, Clutch. Lobster dinner, at my place, the pleasure of my company…get creative," I offered.

"Anything more than dinner?" Clutch asked playfully.

"No!" I stated.

Clutch and I were an item seven years ago when I was working a homicide in Key West and he was using a new drone to assist in the crime scene investigation. We hit it off and had a fling. Soon after, I took a new job as a deputy sheriff in the Mangrove County Sheriff's Department, Clutch took a new job in the Florida Bureau of Investigation, and that was the end of it.

"I may be able to get you one dog, Mutt," Clutch spat out reluctantly.

"One! What the heck, one dog? There are five working in the state! Are they all being used right now?" I asked.

"Yes, but Mutt is done with his job in Key West, and his handler Jaca will be heading back to his home in Miami," Clutch stated.

"Great, but why Mutt?" I asked, curious.

"Because Mutt is the best cadaver dog we have, and he's the only one available," Clutch explained.

"Can he be here at Point Key tomorrow morning around 6:00 a.m.?"

"I'll check and get back to you," said, Clutch warming up a little. "Hey, this is going to cost you more than one lobster dinner at your place." I could hear him smirking.

"More than one lobster dinner?" I asked. "Why?"

"Because I've been meaning to call you and see if we could get together again," said Clutch, his usually confident voice becoming softer. "I miss you."

"Right," I said, trying to process this change in him. "You missed me? Why? You're still crazy about your gadgets, your drones, and your new ground penetrating radar unit. And I hear there's a possibility you may be in for a promotion to assistant director." I was a little nervous and was rambling to fill the silence.

Luckily, the change of subject worked, and Clutch took the bait. "Right, when hell freezes over. I am busy now; can I get back to you shortly?"

"What do I need to do to get that radar unit here?" I asked.

"Find more bodies—at least one or more bodies. Then I may be able to convince the Cocoa Beach Police Chief to move the radar unit down to your location," Clutch said.

"OK," I replied.

He hung up.

Crud, I thought. *Do I want to find more bodies?*

At 7:00 a.m. the next day, Mutt and Officer Jaca arrived at the Hut. Doaks arrived shortly after and began barking orders at me. "Hood, give me an update."

"Well, I've just introduced myself to Officer Jaca and his dog, Mutt," I explained.

"Let's get going," Doaks ordered.

I directed Mutt and Officer Jaca into the Hut and went to the crime scene. Within minutes, Mutt sat down.

"What does that mean?" I asked Officer Jaca. But I was afraid I already knew the answer. "He found another body," Officer Jaca said nonchalantly.

"Another body," Doaks moaned. "Are you kidding me? That dog is wrong. There's no other body there. You are wrong,"

"There is another body buried there!" Officer Jaca snapped.

"Crud," I muttered.

Doaks looked at me and then at the dog. "Go get some shovels, Hood." he ordered.

I went to the Hut's maintenance shed and got two shovels. I returned, kept one and handed the other to Doaks.

"What? I'm not digging in the sand," Doaks uttered, sounding like a spoiled child. "Give it to Officer Jaca."

"I don't dig," declared Officer Jaca with a smirk.

Then Doaks looked at me. "Go for it, superstar!"

I extended the crib and pushed it deeper into the sand. Then I began to dig. Five minutes later, my shovel hit something. I quit shoveling and started clearing the sand around the object. Within seconds, I swept away the sand from the top of a Styrofoam box. It was shaped like a cube, approximately 14" × 14" × 14." The container appeared to be wrapped in duct tape.

"Crud," I whispered to myself.

"Get your knife and cut the tape," Doaks ordered.

"Wait, let me document this scene," I told him calmly. I photographed, diagramed, and completed a rough sketch on this new discovery.

"Now Doaks, please begin to videotape my actions," I directed him. I took out my knife, and slowly began to cut the duct tape sealing the lid on this container. I opened the container and saw another object—a baby blanket. Crud, there was something wrapped in the blanket. I removed the blanket and found a dead baby wrapped in plastic.

"Did you get all of this, Doaks?" I asked.

"Shut up, Hood, of course I did," Doaks said.

"Crud," I stated, "another body. Guess you can call Dr. Spock."

"Wait," Officer Jaca said suddenly. "There's another body there."

What the heck is this? I thought, as a feeling of dread moved through me.

"Another body there?" Doaks asked. "Are you and this dog crazy?"

"No." Officer Jaca was losing his patience with Doaks. "Mutt has not moved; his actions indicate that there is another body located at this scene."

"Well, Hood, keep shoveling," Doaks ordered. *Great* I

thought, *no need for my morning workout today*. I readjusted the crib and started shoveling. Within a few minutes, my shovel hit another object. "Oh no," I whispered, "not again." Once again, I asked Doaks to videotape me. He did, and I began to wipe away the sand from around another object. The top of another container slowly appeared. This container was similar to the shape and size of the other container I had just found, but appeared to be smaller, about a twelve-inch cube. As I cleared the top part of the container, I began to process the crime scene.

Photos, diagrams, and the video should be enough documentation, I thought. Doaks didn't say a word. He let me do all the crime scene processing while videotaping me. Once I cleared all the sand off the box, I noticed that it was also duct taped. I took out my knife and cut the duct tape around the lid. I opened the top and found another blanket. This blanket was smaller than the one in the other container. There was something inside.

"Crud," I said. I slowly opened the blanket and again, there inside the blanket was a baby wrapped in plastic.

Doaks looked on in amazement. "You have got to be kidding me," he blurted in excitement. "Three bodies in the same area. This has to be the work of a serial killer!"

"Let's wait to see what the coroner's office finds out," I said. I did not share his excitement. "Dr. Spock should be here soon. We'll know a lot more once he completes the autopsies on these bodies."

Mutt moved away from where he was sitting and then sat down again, this time closer to the seawall.

"What the heck does this mean?" I asked in amazement.

"What is he doing?" Doaks chimed in.

"Well, I've never seen Mutt do this before," Officer Jaca stated. "I'm not really sure what Mutt is trying to tell us."

Just then, Dr. Spock arrived. Doaks jumped up to meet him. "

"Well Doc, we now have two additional bodies," Doaks said proudly, acting like he dug them up himself.

"Two more bodies?" asked Dr. Spock, dumfounded.

"Yes," replied Doaks, "both appear to be babies buried some time ago."

Dr. Spock looked at the Styrofoam containers, then at the dog, then at Officer Jaca.

"Is that a cadaver dog," Dr. Spock inquired. "Do you think there are more bodies hiding here?"

"Not sure, Doc. I've never seen Mutt act this way before. I need to talk with my cadaver handlers and ask what their thoughts are on this," Officer Jaca was puzzled.

"What are your suggestions for this crime scene?" I asked.

"I would suggest you post a guard at the scene and close the area down until I can find some additional information to explain Mutt's actions," Officer Jaca stated.

Doaks was sitting down and listening to our conversation. "I need to get approval for the overtime on this case from the sheriff," he said. "I think we should let the owners of the Hut know that we're closing them down until further notice."

"OK with me, but they aren't going to be happy with your order," I mumbled as I walked away from Doaks.

By 10:00 a.m., the Hut was shut down indefinitely, Mutt and Officer Jaca were gone, and there was a guard posted at the crime scene and another one posted at the entrance to the Hut.

Doaks and I headed to the morgue.

"How about a McDonald's breakfast?" asked Doaks, looking at me.

"Sure, you can buy," I prodded.

"Shut up Hood, you are the rookie, and rookies always buy," Doaks said.

"Yes, sir," I said.

It was going to be a long day.

Chapter Four: Dr. Spock's Autopsy Report

August 19, 2021
Dr. Spock called me around 10:15 a.m.
"I have a preliminary report on those bodies we found at the Hut," he told me. "Can you and Sgt. Doaks come over this afternoon around 4:00 p.m.?"
"Can you hold on for one minute while I find Doaks and ask him?" I asked.
"Sure," he replied. I took off looking for Doaks. *Where the heck is he?* I wondered. "Doaks, Doaks," I shouted in the squad room, then in the workout area, and then in the bathroom area.
"What do you want now, Hood?" echoed Doaks's voice from inside the men's room.
"Dr. Spock would like to meet with us this afternoon; can you do this?" I asked.

"Hang on a few minutes, let me check my desk calendar. I think I can, but I'm not sure," Doaks replied. Several minutes and one more doughnut later, Doaks told me we could go. I ran back to my desk to see if Dr. Spock was on the line after waiting ten minutes.

"Sorry, I was trying to find Doaks," I responded. "We can meet you at your office today at 4:00 p.m."

"Great, see you then." Dr. Spock hung up.

By 11:30 a.m., Doaks had finished his third doughnut and was sitting at my desk in my chair.

"Hood, what do you think Spock's reports will say?" he asked.

"I'm not sure, but will you please get out of my chair?" I asked him.

"Thanks. Now where are we on our follow-up reports on each of these bodies?" I asked.

Doaks took a long look at me, then at his desk piled high with who knows what. "Let me think for one second, Hood. I think I got all the recent findings from NCIC (National Crime Information Center), Computerized Criminal History (CCH), and from DPS (Department of Public Safety) in Florida on our male subject," Doaks said, reaching for a stack of reports in the middle of his desk.

About five minutes later, after a pile of other things had fallen onto the floor, Doaks handed me a folder—known as the Homicide Book—and told me to review it. I opened it and started to read. Possible name: Jack Kennedy. Caucasian male. Possible date of birth: August 9, 1960. Height: six foot three inches. Weight: 190 pounds. Hair: brown. Slender build, eyes hazel, no marks or tattoos. The victim was identified by putting his fingerprints through the Automatic Fingerprint Identification System (AFIS).

There was an asterisk at the end of the report, meaning that when the original set of fingerprints were taken, the subject had resisted arrest for a shoplifting charge following his eighteenth birthday. In addition to this charge, the NCIC and the DPS reports mentioned that he was a possible suspect in three homicides over the past three decades and was suspected of embezzling millions of dollars from several older women in the Keys. There were five Florida police departments interested in talking to Mr. Jack Kennedy, but none of them were able to identify his residential address over the past thirty years.

The NCIC and DPS reports on the two other bodies—the babies—identified each as male, possibly of Hispanic or Mexican decent. Both had no marks or signs of violence to indicate cause of death. There was nothing else in the DPS or NCIC reports.

"So, Doaks," I asked," did you follow up with these other police departments on their suspicions that Jack Kennedy was involved in other homicides or other related crimes?"

"No," Doaks stated, "I was tied up over the past few days on a special investigation the Chief asked me to do."

"In fact," he continued, "I was hoping to assign you

to do this follow-up work. I'm still tied up with this special investigation. Can you do that, Hood?"

Great I thought, *I'm already working these three homicides, and two more recently came in.*

"Sure," I stated. "I am only working five homicides now!"

"Get used to it," Doaks bellowed at me. "You rookies need as much practical experience as possible!"

Great, here comes another lecture about the great homicide detective Doaks in his early years, I thought.

Thankfully, just as Doaks was about to begin lecture number 568, the chief deputy walked into our office and told Doaks to follow him. Doaks left, and I reviewed the Homicide Book one more time. I took my time and went over each of the DPS findings again. I noted each police department and contact detective's phone number listed. After another hour, I had some more notes. I then started my calls. I wanted to contact as many of these agencies as possible prior to our 4:00 p.m. meeting with Dr. Spock.

By 3:00 p.m., I had contacted four of the five police departments listed in the DPS and NCIC reports. In all four departments, the primary or lead detective had retired and then passed away. Each department had a cold case section; however, the four retired detectives I spoke to could not locate their reports right away due to the thirty-year time gap. I left my name, phone number, and badge number with each detective and asked them to contact me when they could locate their reports and any other information.

I was starving by the time I headed out the door. Just then, Doaks called me. "Hood, I'm hungry. Are you?"

"Yes, I was heading out to get a quick bite before going to Dr. Spock's office," I stated.

"Great, you can drive. Let's go to Momma's diner and grab a quick lunch; their special today is roast beef and mashed potatoes," Doaks said, grabbing his sports coat and heading toward the parking lot. "Let's go. I want to get there before they run out of their special."

Just another day with Doaks. He was more worried about eating than most homicide detectives I'd worked with in the past eight years.

We arrived at Dr. Spock's office right on time. As we were ushered in by the receptionist, Doaks excused himself to search for the men's room.

"It's on your right about five doors down," I instructed him. I'd been through this routine with Doaks every time we'd come here over the past fourteen months. Doaks always seemed to forget where the men's room was located.

Dr. Spock entered his office at 4:05 p.m. "Where's Doaks?" he asked.

"In the men's room," I told him.

"Just great. I am very busy, and I need to go over my preliminary findings on the bodies we recovered. I have two more autopsies pending," he said.

"Let's go ahead; I'll bring Doaks up to speed after we are done," I assured him, and he sat down.

"I will only be giving you a broad overview of my initial report. Spock stated. "There was nothing remarkable about the male subject we found. All his organs were unremarkable considering his age and gender. I sent all body fluids to the DPS crime lab's toxicology section for analysis."

"How long will their analysis take?" I asked.

"Ten weeks to ten months," Spock stated.

"Ten months!" I exclaimed. "Why so long?"

"The DPS Lab, like most crime labs in our country, is understaffed and has a backlog of homicide cases lasting over a year," Spock replied. "This COVID-19 crap has taken its toll on our crime labs and their personnel."

"I understand. We're also down five deputies now with three more retiring next month," I told him.

Spock continued with his initial report. "I found some interesting things I'd like to share with you, Hood. I found several long scratch marks on the back of our victim. I've seen these types of scratches before following some aggressive lovemaking. I believe the male subject may have been poisoned, and I believe these scratches may hold some evidence. But I can't prove it, given what I found during the autopsy."

"What the heck?" I asked.

"I just am speculating here while I wait for the toxicology reports to come back on him," Spock said.

"Can you tell me why you think Jack Kennedy was poisoned?"

"Is that his name? Jack Kennedy?"

"Yes, Doaks got an initial report back from the prints we sent to DPS crime lab yesterday," I told him.

"Interesting," Spock stated, "I heard about a guy with that name being involved in a possible homicide in Key West about twenty years ago."

"Really," I said. "Could we get together and discuss what you know on this case, tomorrow?"

"No," Spock stated, "I'm tied up with yet another autopsy tomorrow and now another three bodies are waiting."

"OK," I stated, "but could I stop by the office later in the week and discuss this case with you?"

"Perhaps," Spock stated, "I don't know what this week will bring, but I will try. "Now Hood," he continued, can you just let me complete my initial report to you?"

"Sorry," I said and shut up for the next fifteen minutes. Spock continued telling me more things he found during Kennedy's autopsy.

"First, I did not find any contents in his stomach. That is very unusual given that his time of death was twenty-four to forty-hours hours before you found him. Over the past ten years of doing autopsies, I've generally found some type of stomach content twenty-four to forty-hours after death. I wondered about the lack of stomach contents and whether a person could empty the stomach contents of a homicide victim without cutting into his abdomen or perhaps use a syringe to suck out the contents. That was my hunch, but there were no puncture wounds around his abdomen area. I then checked his throat. Again, I found nothing significant in his airway to suggest someone may have tried to suck out his stomach contents after his death. I did some more research and contacted a mortician friend of mine to ask him a simple question. After someone dies, could a person hang the body upside down to empty the contents left their stomach? The mortician told me yes, you could simply either hang the body up by the ankles and let the stomach contents drain out onto the floor, or you could put the body over a railing and let the contents of the stomach fall below." Given that information, Spock stated, "I looked for marks along the victim's ankles or along his midsection. Unfortunately, again I found nothing to indicate this was done on our homicide victim. These scratches may also hold some evidence too. I'll wait on the toxicology reports, but I believe these scratches hold some key evidence."

Next, Spock gave me a quick report on the two babies we discovered at the scene. "My initial report is that these two babies were males and either Caucasian, Hispanic, or Mexican. There were no signs of trauma on their bodies, nor did X-rays indicate any signs of violence on their skeletons. These babies were premature, and I cannot tell if they were alive when they were born or stillborn. I sent DNA specimens off to the crime lab to ascertain if we could identify the mothers of these babies. I anticipate these results will be completed sometime in the next year or two."

"The next year or two!" I exclaimed.

"Yes, if not longer." Spock replied. "Our crime labs are not as quick as these private businesses like 23andMe or MyAncestory.Com. DNA analysis for a state-funded crime lab takes years. DNA analysis for bodies deceased for a decade or more is the lowest priority in a crime lab pecking order."

"Years?" I asked. "At this rate, we won't be able to find the mothers of these babies until next year or later. That is not right."

"Well, if you or your department wants to spend an additional thousand dollars to get a private lab to determine these two babies' DNA, then go for it," Spock explained sitting back in his chair and folding his arms.

Spock then told me to quit asking questions and let him finish. He continued telling me that babies were wrapped in two separate blankets and that he found no physical evidence on their bodies. Now he wanted to give our department the two blankets so that we could try to get more information on their deaths.

"Yes, please release them to me this afternoon, and I will begin two other evidence sheets on these two items," I told him.

Spock then stated there was one more thing he was exploring. "Remember how I told you to make sure we had all the contents of the plastic sheet wrapped around the body?"

"Yes," I replied.

"Well, I found this item, I am not sure what it is, but it appears to be some type of leaf." Spock handed me the item to add to our evidence case file sheet. "Can you try to find out what plant has this type of leaf?"

I nodded.

"Time for me to go," Spock said. He then signed off on the new evidence sheets and left.

Ten minutes later, Doaks appeared. "Where is Spock? What did he tell you? How long was his initial briefing?" Doaks asked.

Spock has gone back to perform a few more autopsies," I told him.

"Crap," said Doaks, "was I that long?"

"Yes, you spent over twenty minutes in the restroom," I replied.

OK," Doaks stated, "let's discuss his report at McDonald's where you can buy me a cup of coffee."

Great, I thought, *I'm going to go broke feeding this guy*, and off to McDonald's we went.

Chapter Five: The Reunion of The Lost Sister

Sometime between August 2017 and May 2018
Maria Hernandez had been wondering about a mystery twin sister all her life. As a child, she always asked her mother, her older relatives, and herself one question: "Where is she?" She always sensed that she had a twin out there somewhere.

Maria Hernandez was forty-five years old and had been married to Jose for fifteen years. She was the owner of the Hut and two apartment complexes in the area. Jose had inherited millions of dollars following his parents' death. She made sure she would be extremely rich by manipulating Jose's inheritance and all the money made by the Hut through various fake offshore corporations. She paid Juan Perez, her accountant, $500,000 a year in cash to keep the noses of the IRS and the Florida Department of Revenue out of the Hut's finances.

She also loved men, men who were attractive and wealthy or who possessed something she wanted. Along with her fondness for men, she loved designer drugs.

But Maria's greatest love was her daughter, Salsa. Salsa was the best daughter any mother could have. She and Salsa had become good friends and she had introduced Salsa to her love of drugs and men too. But despite having all these things, for the past forty-five years, she had always felt she was missing someone in her life.

Enough thinking about this. It's time to act, she thought to herself one night. Maria always believed she had a sister. She remembered listening as a small child to her parents and her grandparents speaking in hushed tones about a lost twin.

Her grandmother died in August 2017, leaving behind a lot of family letters and heirlooms. It was during one of her trips to grandmother's home that Maria discovered the truth. In her grandmother's dresser, she found three letters her mother had written.

Her mother had run away from home sixty years ago and had delivered twins—Maria and Selena, her twin sister. The letters between her mother to her grandmother indicated that Maria was kept by the Gonzales family, while Selena was given up to an adoption agency. The letters were what prompted Maria to start a DNA search for her sister.

She went onto Ancestry.com. and spoke to the oldest living relative in the Gonzales family. Finally, the spring of 2018, Maria found her lost twin sister, Selena Rodriquez, living in Spain. She had no memory of her sister since they were separated at birth, but once she found Selena, she called her numerous times. During these phone conversations, she learned that Selena was married and had a job working for the Director of Archivo General de Indies, a maritime museum in Seville. After more phone calls and emails, Selena agreed to meet with Maria to catch up on their separate lives.

In May 2018, Maria flew to Seville to meet Selena for the first time. They had a wonderful time together and made up for lost time discussing each other's families, children, marriages, and businesses. It was during one of these conversations when Maria asked Selena if she would be interested in helping her find a lost shipwreck.

Selena looked interested. "Can I take a look at your research?" she asked Maria.

"Yes, please do," replied Maria and then continued talking as Selena glanced through the materials.

Maria's research indicated the *Santa Isabella* sailed from Cuba in July 1733. The ship was lost in a hurricane. The cargo in this ship was estimated to have over fifty tons of gold, silver, four kilograms of emeralds, and five kilograms of diamonds. According to Maria's research, there had been three recovery efforts on the suspected shipwreck site: however, nothing was found.

"Will you help me find this ship?" Maria asked Selena.

"What is in it for me?" Selena asked hesitantly.

"You are my sister," Maria stated. "We can evenly split

anything we find."

"What kind of experience have you had in looking for shipwrecks?"

"This would be the second time I have put up a lot of money to find a shipwreck in the past decade," Maria confided. "In my first venture I put up $500,000 to find a skilled diver who had experience working on a salvage ship that had found a sunken Spanish galleon called *Nuestra de la Atocha*. After looking for this ship over ten years, Mel Fisher and his crew found it and hauled off $404 million worth of cargo.

"I researched the crew members on Mel Fisher's salvage ship and located a diver named Jack Kennedy. After months of research, I found him living in Key West. I contacted him and invited him to my restaurant for a discussion. He came and after several days of discussion, we agreed to launch our own salvage operation. We began searching for another Spanish galleon call the *Santa Isabella*. Our family had heard rumors for the past hundred years about a sunken treasure ship located off the shoreline of the Hut.

"This ship supposedly sank somewhere near Key Marathon in the 1730s. Jack and I located what we thought was a survivor's story in one of the manifestos in the maritime libraries in the Keys. The library had copies of several manifestos supposedly written in Spanish by prior sea captains or first mates. The librarians had researched the authenticity of and claimed they were validated by the director of Archivo General de Indes. In the manifesto, one of the captains of the recovery ship wrote down the story from two survivors from the *Santa Isabella*. Both survivors claimed they were blown off the ship and hung onto a wooden crate floating in the ocean. They landed on an island with a small cave and stayed there for three days. By the third day, the hurricane had passed, and they went outside. The survivors story indicated that the ship was lying in sixty feet of water, so her top masts were visible from shore. Two months later, the survivors were rescued by another Spanish ship and taken back to Cuba. There, the governor launched three rescue attempts to find the *Santa Isabella*. After six months, the rescue operations were stopped and the ship was not found."

"Given this information," Maria continued, "I gave Jack $500,000 to buy a salvage ship, hire a crew, and start plotting where he thought the ship may be located. I also did my own research. I became very good friends with several weathermen, an oceanographer, and a climatologist. Using their suggestions, I believed we could plot where the *Santa Isabella* is located. All of this information pointed to a location in the Atlantic Ocean off the shoreline of the Hut."

Maria then told Selena they had started the search. "But it did not last long. Jack's crew all got very sick with a virus. Then the boat burned at sea. During the next six months, Jack and I did more research, and he wanted to start again. But he wanted $2 million to begin this new search. Once I told him no, he left."

"Now I need your help," Maria told Selena. "I believe

you have access to records of this ship and others. With your help, we can begin a new search around the Key Marathon Islands. I also believe if you can do your research in the Archivo, I can coordinate your findings with some ongoing research I have just located in my area."

Selena thought about Maria's request. She had always been fascinated with shipwrecks, and she knew the Archivo's records could hold more critical information.

After a few minutes of silence, Selena nodded. "Yes," I will help you."

The twin sisters hugged each other.

"It feels good to have a sister and even better to have a sister willing to work on a family project," Maria said.

Over the next two years, Maria collected more information on how to locate the current position of the *Santa Isabella,* aided by the information Selena found in her Archivo research. She also studied hurricanes and other weather data and looked at how these changed the ocean's current patterns. Given some recent oceanic data on how major hurricanes impacted the ocean currents around the Keys in the last fifty years, she began researching the impact of fifty hurricanes that had occurred in this area since 1733. She was convinced that she could use this data to project the new location of the *Santa Isabella.* To augment her ocean and weather research, Maria located and interviewed a number of the salvage crew members from the *Atocha* discovery. She had also recently found a new source of oceanic information on hydrodynamics and eddies in Mr. Shane Moldune, a marine engineer.

She called Selena up one afternoon. "Do you feel we have enough information to put some substantial money into a new salvage operation to find the *Santa Isabella*?"

"How much money are we going to invest to get this search started?" Selena asked.

"My estimates is between $1.5 and 2.5 million," Maria replied.

"Maria," asked Selena, "where are we going to get that kind of money?"

Maria then told Selena how she had managed to hide millions of dollars in several offshore accounts.

"I can get us up to 3 million in one week if we need it," she told Selena confidently. Selena let out a huge sigh. "You have access to that kind of money?"

"Yes, and more when we need it. So what do you think? Should we begin our new search or not?" Maria asked.

Selena was silent for a few seconds. "Yes, let's begin. So, where is Jack?"

Chapter Six: The Hunt for Jack Kennedy

April 2016

In May 2016, she located and proceeded to become very friendly with Jack. He had a reputation as one of the best treasure hunters in the Keys, if not the whole world.

Maria invited Jack to the Hut to discuss her dream of finding a sunken treasure ship. She and Jack were immediately attracted to each other. Jack was forty years old, 6'3 tall, and in excellent physical shape. Maria was forty years old, 5'3, and had a body shaped like an hourglass. During their six-month business relationship, Jack and Maria spent a lot of time together in Maria's private apartment adjacent to the Hut. Their physical relationship was excellent, but their business partnership was not. There was a lot of mystery around this one ship. Maria had found only one reference to it during her extensive research in two maritime museums.

She found the name of this ship in a side story relating to a secret mission from the King of Spain in 1732. She guessed where this ship sailed from and when it sailed. Her research was then given a little more credibility when she found another story about two survivors from the ship called *Isabella*.

Jack had convinced Maria he had discovered the location of this ship using the same data Mel Fisher's crew used in locating the *Atocha* shipwreck. Maria reviewed Jack's research and then agreed to give him $500,000 to start the hunt. Unfortunately, during the first month of Jack's search, his crew got sick with the flu and then his ship caught fire. The treasure hunting venture failed only six weeks after it had begun.

By January 2020, Maria had shared her recent findings about the mystery ship *Isabella* with Selena. Selena also found more information on several Spanish sunken ships in the Point Key area. The ship called the *Nuestra Senora de Isabella* appeared to have been on a secret mission. Selena located some correspondence between King Philip V to a Dr. Burnet in Havana, Cuba. The date of their correspondence was June 1732. Dr. Burnet was part of the South Sea company operating in Havana at this time, and he was directed by the king to smuggle a cargo of gold, silver, jewelry, and slaves on the ship called *Isabella*. The king paid Dr. Burnet several hundred pounds of gold and silver for his services and told Burnet that Special Captain Ernesto Diego was sailing from the port of

Barcelona to Havana. The captain was sworn to secrecy by the king himself. In this correspondence, Selena found that the King wanted to start a new bank to limit the financial control his second wife had on him. The correspondence indicated the ship was to sail from Havana to Barcelona in June 1733. Selena noted there was no other research on this ship nor on its secret mission.

Several months later, Selena did find a note on this ship's name attached to another ship's log. In October 1733, another ship's log indicated there were two survivors from the *Nuestra Senora de Isabella*. The survivors' story recorded in the captain's log indicated the *Isabella* had sunk in a hurricane. The survivors stated they were near the "*metacumbres*" (islands) when their ship sank. They stated the ship had sunk in a hurricane in June 1733. Both stated the island they were on had a small cave that protected them from the hurricane until they were rescued by this ship. Their stories were recorded in Barcelona once their rescue ship reached this port in October 1733. Selena said she searched an additional three months trying to locate more information, but found nothing.

Given this new research, Maria decided to renew her search for this ship. She recalled that there was a small cave on Point Key when her family first came to Key Marathon. She began her second search to find Jack Kennedy again. She believed Jack was the best candidate to head up another shipwreck venture. She found out that he was still in the treasure business, but there was no current information on his location. She continued her search and found that his last known location was in Bermuda. She also learned that he was going through his third divorce when his wife filed a missing person's report with the Miami Police Department. There were also several collections agencies trying to locate him for late alimony payments.

Having limited luck finding Jack, Maria expanded her search by contacting some of his old friends. She learned from these friends that Jack was hiding from the federal government for unpaid income taxes, from the state of Florida for unpaid state taxes, and was in hundreds of thousands of dollars in debt in alimony payments to his three former wives. Maria kept digging and found the name of Jack's best friend—a woman named Dawn White. Dawn had worked with Jack as a crew member on the *Atocha* adventure in 1985. They were great friends and probably had an intimate relationship during their eighteen months on Mel Fisher's ship. Maria found Dawn's old phone number, which Jack had given her in 2016. She called that number, only to find that it was disconnected. She continued her search and found an old National Geographic picture listing Dawn's last name following the *Atocha* find. She searched Google again for Dawn's last name, and after calling fifteen different Dawn Whites, she believed she had finally located the right one.

"Hello Ms. White, I am a friend of Jack Kennedy," Maria stated. "I was wondering if I could talk to you regarding Jack."

"How do I know you are who you say you are?" the person replied.

"Do you remember your time with Mel Fisher and his crew on the hunt for the *Atocha*, when you were very close to Jack?" Maria asked. "I know this information because I hired Jack to find a sunken treasure ship for me in 2016. He talked about you all the time."

"Well, the son of a gun left me with a child, and no child support," the person stated. "In fact, if I knew where he was, I would go after him myself to collect the $100,000 he owes me in back child support."

"What if I could pay you part of this money to find Jack?" Maria asked.

"What is your name again?" the caller asked.

"Maria Hernandez. I live in Point Key," Maria replied.

"If you are serious about finding Jack, meet me in Captain Hooks Bait parking lot in thirty minutes," said the caller.

"OK," Maria stated. "I will see you there in thirty minutes."

She changed clothes and left the Hut. Fifteen minutes later, she arrived at the bait shop and parked her car in one of the twenty empty spaces and then waited. Two minutes later, a tall, slender woman in a short sundress and carrying a large purse slipped into her passenger seat.

"Are you Maria Hernandez?" the woman asked.

"Yes, and you are Dawn," Maria replied.

"That depends; I need to get some more information

about your request," replied the passenger. "First, tell me why you want to find Jack and how you found me."

"Jack and I were business partners in 2016, he and I attempted to locate a sunken ship around Point Key. The partnership failed after his crew got sick with the flu and the boat caught on fire and sank. During this time, Jack and I had several discussions about the *Atocha*, how it was found, what instruments were used in locating this ship after 300 years in the Gulf, and we also talked a lot about you."

"Listen, I know a lot about you and Jack, since we shared a lot of personal information during our time together," Maria continued. "I just need to find him and see if he's interested in another search for another sunken ship."

"What is in it for me?" the woman asked.

"A lot, if you agree to help me find him," Maria replied.

"I want specifics. Like how much money would I get up-front if we find him? How much money would I get if I help you and him and we find this treasure?" the woman asked.

"That amount depends on what type of information you can give me in the next few hours," Maria said. "I know Jack may be living in Bermuda, and I know he is in a lot of financial trouble with the state and federal governments and his three ex-wives. If you have any information on where he is now, and if I can contact him in the next two hours, we'll talk money."

"You still haven't answered my question," the woman stated and began to exit the car.

"OK, just hold on one minute," Maria pleaded. "For starters, how about $25,000 if you stay with me here in the car, and I call the number you have in your purse?

"I want $50,000.00 cash first. Then I'll give you the number and you'll agree to keep me as a partner in your treasure hunt," the woman proposed.

"Why should I give you anything?" Maria asked. "You haven't given me one thing yet that indicates who you are!"

"Listen, I'm here, and we're talking, which is better than what you had about two hours ago," the woman insisted.

"True, but this is getting us nowhere," Maria countered. "Just tell me what you want to get started."

"First, I know you are Maria Hernandez," said the woman. "I have a picture of you here in my purse. Next, I know about your relationship with Jack; he left you and came to live with me in Key West for a few months until he got his own business going.

"So here's my deal," she continued. "I want to find that guy and force him to pay me $50,000 in child support. I know where he is right now, because two months ago, I took my son, and went to Bermuda to find him. I found his home, and his business; however, he wasn't there, and no one knew when he had left.

"Typical Jack," she continued, "he has a sixth sense about when the feds, or his ex-wives, or I would show up on his doorstep demanding money. So, what are you going to do? Trust me or blow me off?"

Maria thought about this conversation. Fifteen minutes of talk with no solid proof of who this woman was and if she was saying anything truthful.

"Get out of the car," Maria ordered. "Go now. You haven't given me any information I don't already have or know, so leave."

"OK," the woman stated. She then pulled out her clutch purse and showed Maria her Florida driver's license with her picture.

"Dawn White," Maria read.

"Pleasure to meet you too," Dawn chuckled. "Now can we stop all of this crap and get to work?"

"Maybe," Maria said. "If you want any money, I want his exact location in Bermuda and his phone number right now."

"OK, but I want some type of deal. Got it?" Dawn demanded.

"All right, this is my deal for you," Maria began. "First, if his location and his phone number check out, I'll wire $25,000 to your bank account on Wednesday. Next, if I can locate Jack and if he agrees to come back to Florida with me, you can work with us as a business partner."

OK, that's a start, but what about my cut of any treasure we find?"

"If we find Jack and he comes back to Point Key and agrees to help us locate this sunken ship, I'll give you 10 percent of anything we find."

"I want at least 15 percent of anything you find."

"Dawn, you are not in a good position to negotiate anything," Maria told her. "You are desperate for money to feed your kid, and you are behind in most of your utility bills and house payments. Don't give me your demands. Either take my offer or leave now."

Dawn hesitated and then said, "OK, I'll take it."

"Good, now give me Jack's cell phone number and his location in Bermuda," Maria said.

"Once the money is in my account, I'll give you the information," Dawn said. Then she was out of the car and gone.

Where did she go? What the heck is this? thought Maria. She looked around and, strangely enough, she didn't see another car or another person in the parking lot. *Was she a ghost or what? Well, I'll wire the money into this account on Wednesday, but I'll verify every piece of information she gave me.*

On Wednesday morning at 12:01 a.m., Maria transferred $25,000 into the account number Dawn White gave her.

At 12:05 a.m., she got a phone call.

"Hello, Dawn?" Maria asked.

"Yes, it is Dawn. Thanks for wiring me the money," she said. "Jack's phone number is (441) 421-1111. His address is 2203 Long Street, Hamilton, Bermuda."

"OK, I will get back to you in fifteen minutes. Are you going to be at this number?" asked Maria.

"Yes. When you call Jack, expect the phone to ring at least

eleven times, then expect a beep to leave a message, or Jack may unexpectedly answer the phone," Dawn advised Maria.

"Thanks, I will get back to you," Maria said and hung up.

She waited a few minutes to think about what just occurred. *Perhaps I should call my police friend, James,* I thought. James Jose was a dispatcher at the Mangrove County Sheriffs Communication Center. He was a family cousin and had given her some valuable information she needed about various people over the past fifteen years.

She called James on his cell phone with a 911 following her number. He returned the call within a minute.

"Maria, what do you need?" he asked.

"James, I need you to verify a phone number in Bermuda. Can you do this now?"

"Not now but give me a few minutes. I'll call you back, OK?"

"Sure, I just need to have this checked out ASAP, and I'll see you on Sunday at Salsa' party," Maria said.

Five minutes later, James called back and verified that the number belonged to a Mr. Jack Kennedy.

"Thanks," Maria said. "See you on Sunday."

She started to work on her game plan to get Jack back into her life.

She called the phone number. Only after it had rung ten times did she realize it was 12:45 a.m. in Bermuda. She prayed he would answer.

"Hello," answered a woman's voice. "Who is this?"

"Hi, this is Maria. Is Jack Kennedy there?"

"Please wait while I get him," the woman said.

A few seconds later, a male voice stated, "Hello, how can I help you?"

"Hello, my name is Maria Hernandez. I need to speak to Mr. Jack Kennedy if he's available."

There were a few seconds of nothing. "Please tell me your name again," said the male voice.

"Maria Hernandez, and if this is Jack, quit messing with me and let me talk. If not, get Jack on this phone in three seconds or you'll lose your chance of getting rich," Maria said.

"If this is Maria Hernandez, please describe the tattoo you have on your left thigh," the male voice said.

Maria loved this tattoo, and only a very few men knew about it.

"It's a tiny lobster," Maria said with a chuckle.

"Maria, this is Jack, I need to be sure who you are and why you're calling me at this hour," he replied.

"I understand," Maria stated. "Listen, Jack, I need you to come back to the Hut as soon as possible. I would like to share some research I have been doing with my lost twin sister, and we would like to propose another business venture to find a sunken ship."

Maria hung up the phone then looked out her ocean view apartment window. *Why am I doing this again*? She thought to herself.

Two minutes later, she called Dawn and told her she had

made contact with Jack and that she'd call her later in the week with more information.

Good news, she thought, *I have found Jack, and he will lead me to my treasure.*

Chapter Seven: Salsa's problem

August 13, 2021

At 12:00 p.m. sharp, Maria's cell phone vibrated.

"Hello," she said "Who is this?"

"Maria, this is Jack. I'm running to catch a flight to Miami in a few minutes and then flying to Key West," Jack stated. "Can you pick me up at the airport around six o'clock tonight?"

"Sure, see you soon." Maria hung up and began to plan. She needed to get Jack here as soon as possible so that she could quiz him on his updated research on treasure hunting in the Keys. She wondered what he knew about underwater drones, AUVs, and the laws involving international waters around Key Marathon.

"Crap," she said suddenly, "I have an audit this afternoon at 3:00 p.m. There is no way I can meet Jack at the airport."

Who can I send to get Jack? she thought. *Salsa, she would love meeting Jack. I'll get her to pick him up and bring him here this evening. But I must be careful with Salsa; she is twenty-five and a lot like me. Jack is a good-looking man, and she may think about taking him to her bed. Well, tough, I need to get Jack here ASAP.*

At 6:05 p.m., Jack Kennedy steps off the jet and onto the passenger stairway at the Key West Airport. It was hot, muggy, and very humid. As he approached the passenger terminal, he scanned the awaiting crowd, searching for Maria.

"Nuts," he said, "Maria is not here!" As he approached the terminal, he noticed another attractive woman who looked like a younger version of Maria.

I wonder who that woman is and if she is related to Maria, Jack thought.

"Hello, Mr. Kennedy?" Salsa asked.

"Yes, I am Jack Kennedy," Jack stated. "And you must be Maria's daughter, I guess."

"Yes, my name is Salsa, I am Maria's daughter. Do you have any luggage?"

"No, just my backpack," Jack replied.

"Great," Salsa said. "Then let's get my car and head up the Keys to the Hut."

The drive up to the Hut lasted about an hour and fifteen minutes. There was only one highway up and down the Keys. Given the number of little towns and their police departments, there were speed traps all along the road.

After making some small talk with Jack, Salsa asked him, "What are your thoughts on my mother's plans to find a sunken ship?"

"Well," Jack stated. "I have done a lot of research since your mom called me last night. I think her information from Selena and her updates on the hurricanes and the currents in the Atlantic may provide us with a great starting point to locate the *Isabella*."

"Wow, you are really serious about this treasure hunt," Salsa observed.

"Yes, I am. In fact, my research into the new equipment available to help us find the Isabella is a lot better than the first venture I did with your mother.

"Are you married?" Salsa asked.

"No," Jack stated. "I am single, and I love meeting new and attractive woman. And you are both new and attractive."

Salsa felt an unusual flush come over her body. *What the heck is going on here?* she thought. *He is an attractive man, and Mom always talked about him.*

"Well, here we are," Salsa said, dropping him off at the entrance to the Hut.

"Hey," Jack said, "here is my cell phone number. I would love to have a drink or dinner with you."

Wow, he is something else, Salsa thought.

"OK," she said, "I might contact you in the future."

"Thanks for the ride and the conversation," Jack said as he entered the front door of the Hut.

As soon as Jack entered the Hut, a young man asked him if his name was Jack Kennedy.

"Yes," Jack replied.

"Great, my name is Juan," the young man said. "Ms. Maria asked that you join her in her private apartment next door. Jack follows the young man from the Hut and to the adjacent high rise apartment complex.

"Please," the young man stated. "Ms. Maria would like you to join her in her penthouse suite. Floor number five." He punched the button and left Jack alone in the elevator.

As soon as the elevator door opened, there stood Maria, looking as attractive as she had six years ago. She didn't have many wrinkles or age marks. She looked great.

"Hello, Jack," she murmured. "I've been planning this rendezvous for a long time, and I am anxious to pick up where we left off."

The next morning, Jack woke up to a hot sunny day with a cool ocean breeze coming in from the outside patio facing the Atlantic Ocean.

Wow, what a nice reunion we had last night, Jack thought as he headed into the shower. *Maria has not changed at all; she is just wonderful. I wonder what today will bring.*

After Jack finished showering, he found a note on the dresser in the bedroom. It was written in Maria's elegant handwriting: "When you get up, look in the refrigerator. There are two egg burritos and fresh coffee in the carafe on the oven. Please come down to the pool by the Hut when you're finished with breakfast."

As Jack entered the Hut, every woman in the area stopped what they were doing and looked at him. Maria watched from the bar.

"Jack doesn't know how attractive he is, even at this stage of his life," Maria thought to herself, chuckling. *Eat your heart out, ladies. This man is mine, and I won't let any of you try to seduce him while he is here.*

Maria waited until Jack found a lounge down by the shoreline. Once he lay down, she approached him from the back. He did not see her coming, but as soon as she could, she let the condensation from her drink land on his face.

"Hey," Jack stated. Then he looked up and saw Maria standing there in her thong monokini, laughing at him.

"Try this," she said, handing him the drink, "it's my new energy drink. You need to increase your stamina for our afternoon planning session."

Jack took the drink and watched Maria leave.

She is still attractive as ever, Jack thought. *I am looking forward to our afternoon planning session.*

At 3:00 p.m., Jack met Maria in her penthouse. She was dressed and ready to start planning to find the *Isabella*.

Jack took out his iPad from his backpack and let Maria see his latest research. For the next thirty minutes, he explained to Maria the type of boat, the forms of underwater drones, AUVs, and new scuba gear he researched to find the *Isabella* in the Atlantic.

"Finding the *Isabella* in the Atlantic, will be deeper and totally different than finding the Atocha in the Gulf," Jack explained. "The Atlantic is much deeper, and the wreck site will be harder to find once the ship is found."

Maria was amazed by Jack's extensive research. Jack told her he had found some new research done by a young marine engineer, Shane Moldune, who had been studying the currents around the Keys for the past five years. He examined the NOAA (National Oceanic and Atmospheric Administration) charts involving the impact of various storms and hurricanes in the Keys. Moldune found that the eddies surrounding the Keys created ocean tornadoes moving sand and objects around these islands. He had studied the hydrodynamics of the oceans where he found that some storms can cause underwater tornados that pick up anything in their paths and move them hundreds of feet, yards, or even miles away from their original ocean floor spot. He produced a formula involving the movement of sunken vessels following the eddies around an island applying the hydrodynamics of a hurricane. Moldune had just begun publishing his formulas in scientific journals.

"I think this person has the key to finding the *Isabella*," Jack told Maria. "I have applied his formula to the data you sent me on the *Isabella*. I believe I can now calculate where it moved over these past 300 years."

"Now," he turned and looked at her "what is your proposal to me about finding this ship?"

Maria was expecting this. "I was planning on giving you $2 million to start and an additional $2 million to fund our initial search. Once we locate the *Isabella*, I'll give you 20 percent of the find," she proposed.

Jack looked at Maria for several seconds.

"Twenty percent! Are you crazy?" Jack asked indignantly.

"No," Maria told him. "My sister and I have worked on this project for over three years. Selena has had to research this project very extensively and her information is critical in identifying the location of this ship. Plus, she and I have done 99 percent of the work on this venture. What have you done to contribute to our project over the past three years?"

Jack was surprised at Maria's statements. He knew she had a point. He thought about his response and chose his next words carefully:

"Can we discuss this over an afternoon drink?"

"Not yet," Maria said. "I am not in the mood to negotiate with you on this project. We have all the information we need to start, and your role here is to be my project director. You cannot have any more than what I tell you! Take it or leave now."

Crap, Jack thought. *She is right, she and Selena have done all the work.*

"OK," Jack stated. "You are right, you deserve to have the majority of the credit for this find, and you deserve to have the rights to any treasure we find."

"But?" Maria replied.

"I will work for you, but I cannot guarantee any results until you, me, and Selena review all the research you've done."

Maria was expecting this too. She and Selena had only given a very small amount of the research on the *Isabella* to Jack over the past twenty-four hours. Maria did not trust anyone, and she especially did not trust Jack with any more information.

"When can we all talk about your research?" Jack asked.

"I am not sure when," Maria replied. "I have to go talk to my husband about a new renovation project at the Hut."

She then left the penthouse.

Nuts, Jack thought. *Maria has thought about everything on this new project. I have nothing to add but a small amount of equipment research. Perhaps I can still negotiate a bigger amount if I find a way to attack her personally.*

Jack then left the dining area and went to the bar. There, he poured a double gin and tonic. He needed to buy some time on this negotiation process, and he needed to find a way to attack Maria to shake her confidence on this project. Three drinks later, he thought of a plan.

Maria had a daughter, Salsa. Perhaps I can seduce her, and she can negotiate with her mother about my reward. Jack thought back to a few decades ago when he was in a similar position with another woman like Maria. This woman had done her research too. She had a lot of critical information, and she had set out her demands just like Maria. Jack had kidnapped this woman's son and sent her a ransom note. The woman ended up paying Jack the ransom and never reported the incident to the police.

Perhaps I can create a similar situation here, Jack thought. *What fun. Salsa is a very attractive woman, and if I can get her into bed, she may agree to help me renegotiate with her mother.*

At 5:00 p.m., Jack called Salsa.

"Hello?"

"Hello, Salsa. This is Jack Kennedy."

"Well, hello there, Jack," Salsa said brightly. "I was just thinking about calling you to see if you could join me for drinks tonight at my place."

"Sure, where do you live? And what time should I be there?"

"Can you come over in an hour? I live about two blocks from the Hut, at 202 Fifth Street."

"Great, shall I bring a bottle of wine or a bottle of liquor?" Jack asked.

"No, you just need to bring yourself, and plan on staying the night," Salsa murmured.

Hmm, Jack thought, *she is just like her mother.*

At 5:45 p.m., Jack left a note on the bed in Maria's penthouse and headed toward the

elevator. He hit the button, and as the door opened, there was Maria.

"Going somewhere?" Maria asked.

"Yes," Jack replied. "I am looking at some property on the other side of Key Marathon, and I have a dinner date with a realtor."

"Well, don't be too late. I'd like to follow up our discussion on the *Isabella* later this evening in my bedroom," Maria said.

"Sure."

At 6:05 p.m., Jack walked up to the door at 202 Fifth Street. Just as he was about to ring the doorbell, the door opened.

Come in," Salsa said. Jack entered the house, and there was Salsa, dressed—well, almost dressed—in a very attractive lounge outfit that just covering certain parts of her body.

"Welcome, Jack. Please come in, and let's have a drink," Salsa said.

The drinks were still on the bar an hour later when Jack and Salsa decided to take a pause in their lovemaking.

"Nice," Salsa said breathily. "You have excellent skills in making love to a woman."

"Well," Jack said, smiling, "years of experience."

Over the next few hours, Jack and Salsa continued to enjoy each other's company.

Jack waited until Salsa left her bed to return with another round of drinks before he asked her what she thought of her mother's treasure ship venture.

"My mom is obsessed with this treasure ship thing. She has talked about it all of my life, and now that she has found her lost twin sister, she is addicted to finding this ship," Salsa replied. "I'm sick of hearing about this; all she talks about is the *Isabella, Isabella, Isabella*."

"What are your feelings about her obsession?" Jack asked again.

"I want it ended," Salsa replied. "If I could get her mind off that ship for one day, I would give up one month's pay!"

"What if I could help you get her mind off of this ship for several days?" Jack asked.

"How are you going to do that?" Salsa asked.

"If you could help me, I think we could distract your mom's attention from the *Isabella* to you."

"What do you have in mind?"

"I was thinking of having you tell your mom that you are being blackmailed by a local drug dealer."

"How would that work?" Salsa asked.

"Well, tell your mom that you're behind on a repayment arrangement you had with this drug dealer and he's threatened to carve your face up if you do not repay him by Friday," Jack proposed.

"Interesting idea, since I've just tried some new drugs and Mom likes them too. We may have a plan here," Salsa stated, "but what's in it for me?"

"I need to get your mother to rethink the amount of money she's willing to pay me to find this ship. If we can get her distracted for a while, she may reconsider my worth in this venture," Jack said.

"So, what do I get out of all of this?" Salsa asked.

"What do you want out of it?" Jack asked.

DR. H

Salsa went to the bar, made more drinks, and hopped back in bed.

"I need to get out of this marriage," she stated. "Jairo my husband, is more interested in making money than he is in making me happy as a wife."

"OK," Jack stated. "I have a plan, but I need your full cooperation and it will cost you a little pain and heartache for a while."

"I don't care. I am ready to get out of this marriage, and I want a new life as a single, rich woman," Salsa exclaimed. "Now tell me what I need to do to get your plan going."

Jack's mind raced he puts together two parts of a plan. The first part dealt with the drug dealer. The second part dealt with getting Salsa out of her marriage.

He fills Salsa in. "First, you need to be 100 percent committed to convincing your mother that your life is in grave danger unless you repay this drug dealer. Next, I need to rough you up a little bit. I need you to have some marks on your face, your eyes, and your body to convince your mother that this drug guy is serious and that it'll be worse next time if you do not repay him. Then you need to go call your mom over, show her your marks, and beg her to give you $50,000 in cash. We can work together later to make up a story about the drug dealer suddenly leaving the Keys."

Salsa looked at Jack for a while.

"What about Jairo? How do you intend to get me out of my marriage?" Salsa asked.

"That depends on you. Do you want to divorce Jairo or just leave him?" Jack responded.

Salsa thought for a few minutes. "I don't know what I want to do with him," she admitted. "Can I have some time to think about it?"

"Sure, we can have another planning session in a few days if you don't mind," Jack stated. "But are you sure you can do this?"

"Yes, I need to start over, get a new life, and get my mother back to reality," Salsa insisted.

"OK, then let's have another drink and pick up where we left off…" Jack said as he reached over to Salsa.

The next day, Salsa and Jack were ready with their drug dealer plan. Salsa had let Jack hit her face and her body. Nothing serious, just enough to shift Maria's attention from the *Isabella* to Salsa.

Jack looked at Salsa. "Not too bad. Does it hurt a lot?" he asked.

"No, it looks worse than it feels," Maria said.

"OK, let me get out of here. Wait a little while and then call your mom. Cry a lot, and act hysterical," Jack ordered.

"OK," Salsa stated.

As Jack left Salsa's apartment, he walked back to the Hut, there he was met at the elevator by Maria.

"Where have you been?" she asked.

"My realtor wanted to show me a few condos available on this island," he replied.

"Did the realtor show you anything else?"

"I refuse to answer your question on the grounds it would incriminate me." Jack retorted.

"Fine," Maria stated and began to walk away. Just then, her phone vibrated. She looked at the caller ID.

Crap, it is Salsa. What does she want now? Maria thought.

"Hello, my dear," Maria said.

"Mom, mom, I need to talk to you. I am in trouble, big trouble, and I need your help now!" Salsa yelled over the phone.

"Salsa, please slow down. Take a deep breath, and tell me what's going on," Maria urged.

On the of verge of hysterics, Salsa told her mom about her drug dealer beating her up for not paying her debt. Maria was furious. She instructed Salsa to stay home and told her she was coming right away. While Maria was hitting the elevator call button again, Jack walked over.

"Anything wrong?" he asked.

Maria grabbed his arm. "Salsa is in trouble! I need your help! Can you come with me now?"

"Sure," Jack stated, feigning ignorance. "Where does Salsa live?"

Jack and Maria hurried down to Maria's car and left the Hut. It was a one-minute drive to Salsa's house. They exited Maria's vehicle and hurried to her door. It was open. Maria and Jack rushed in to find Salsa on the floor, crying hysterically and holding a large ice bag to her face. Maria ran over to her daughter and cradled her in her arms.

"Who did this?" Maria demanded. Salsa sobbed for another few minutes.

"Mom," she cried. "I need your help! I need it now or my face and body will be carved up by Diego!"

"Diego? That no-good piece of human flesh!" Maria yelled. "Diego did this to you?"

Yes," Salsa said through her tears, "and he promises it will be worse the next time if I don't pay him the $50,000 I owe him."

"What did you get from him that cost $50,000?"

"Listen mom. He asked me to be his business partner and promised me a 300 percent return on this investment. He told me these new drugs would be the latest craze for the kids in the Keys," Salsa cried. "I thought it was a great way to earn some more money, so I wrote him a check. I forgot to put my slush fund money into the checking account, and the check bounced. Diego was with his business partners when he found out I had no money, and the check was worthless."

She continued sobbing. "Diego was really mad and told me that he needed that money by this evening, or my face and body would be carved up! Mom, can you help me? What should I do? Please mom, what should I do?"

She collapsed into her mother's arms and continued to sob.

Maria thought about the next steps to take. *How can I get Salsa out of this mess, and how can I deal with that scumbag*

Diego? All these questions were floating around in her head. Maria looked down at Salsa. *She's a beautiful, younger version of me. How did she get so pretty and why does she continue to get involved in these bad business deals with these bad men? Lots of questions*, Maria thought, *but no good solutions.*

Salsa stirred in Maria's arms and then looked at Jack.

"Mom, can Jack help us?" She asked. Maria looked over at Jack, who was kneeling by them.

"Jack, could you handle this situation for us?" Maria pleaded.

Jack looked at both women and thought for a few seconds. "I can handle Diego, but I need more information and I need to get a weapon," he stated.

Maria grabbed his arm. "No problem, I can get everything you need." She then tried to coax Salsa up from the floor onto the couch.

As she was moving Salsa, Jack went to the kitchen and got both women a drink of water.

"Here," he said, handing the glasses to Maria and Salsa. "Perhaps this will help."

Both women took the water glasses and drank. "Thanks."

"Now," said Maria, looking at Salsa, "let's go over the whole story on your business deal so Jack and I can get a better picture on what we are about to deal with."

Salsa, still sobbing a little, took a deep breath and explained the business deal to them. Once she was done, both Jack and Maria look at each other and then at Salsa.

"Mom," Salsa asked, "can you get me $50,00 by this evening?"

"Sure, that is no problem," assured Maria. "The problem is what are we going to do about Diego."

Jack was silent for a long time, trying to think of a plan.

"What kind of information do you have on Diego?" he finally asked. "Like where does he do his business, where does he live, does he carry any guns, does he have any muscle with him, and what does his daily schedule look like?"

Maria looked at Salsa and then back at Jack. "Are you sure you can handle this? Diego is bad news. He's wanted in several states and has a reputation for making his enemies disappear."

"Maria, in my treasure hunting experience, I have had to take on some tough people; some had to disappear too. I think Diego and I should have a meeting," Jack suggested. "Can you set something up in a few hours?"

How could that Diego hurt my Salsa? Maria thought. *I am going to kill that guy myself!*

Jack then looked at the women. "We need to get a plan of action started, and we need to start now if we are going to get Diego out of the picture by tonight."

"My dear, we will take care of this," Maria said, caressing Salsa's hair. "Why don't you go to bed and rest awhile. Let Jack and I discuss our options, OK?"

Salsa got up and gave Maria a huge hug. Then she hugged Jack. "How did I do?" she whispered in his ear.

Jack looked down at her and gave her a quick wink. Salsa then left the room.

Maria turned to Jack. "I need a drink; how about you?"

"Sure," Jack agreed, and Maria went off to the bar to fix a drink.

Dang, Jack thought to himself, *where is my necklace?* His necklace was a gold coin on a gold braided chain, both taken from the *Atocha. Dang, where is that thing?* He wondered, rubbing his neck.

"Crap, I wonder if I lost it while Salsa and I were enjoying each other's company in her bedroom?"

Maria came back from the bar holding two drinks. "Here you go. A double gin and tonic."

"Thanks," Jack said, taking a big swallow. "Great job Maria," he said, patting her backside.

"OK, Jack, what do you need from me to get rid of Diego?" Maria asked.

Jack's mind was racing. *I need a lot more information than what you two have given me,* he thought.

"Well," Jack hesitated, "tell me everything you know about this Diego person. Where does he live, does he have any type of business schedule, how do you contact him, and would he be willing to meet with you and I for another business drug deal?"

"Diego is a small man who likes his women and his drugs," Maria said. "He does not have any business schedule. He meets his clientele and provides them with great drugs.

I can arrange a meeting with him in a few hours, but he usually has one or two bodyguards. How are we going to handle them?"

"That depends on you," Jack said. "Can you distract them away from Diego while I convince him he needs to come with us to collect his $50,000?"

"Sure, I can make that happen very easily," Maria assured Jack. "What is your plan once we have him in the car?"

"My plan is to get his two goons away from him and get into his car once you distract them. Once in his car, I'll have him drive out of the area. I'll tell him we are going to your apartment to pick up his money. But I will have him detour along the way and end up in a very secluded beach area on the south side of Marathon." Jack said.

"Perhaps you should drive," he suggested. "I don't know where I am going, and I might need to convince Diego to be a good boy or I'll ruin his male anatomy."

"I love the way you think," Maria said. "My type of man, always considering sex in everything you do." She slowly ran her hands down his stomach.

Jack grabbed her hand and looked into her eyes.

"We need to get a better plan together if we're going to eliminate Diego. Sex can come later," he said.

"Yes, of course," Maria agreed. Then she got up to check on Salsa.

Crap, Jack thought, *I was not planning on killing someone. Well, life throws you a lot of curve balls; this one happens to be a little outside of the box. This isn't the first time someone has had to die. I just need to figure a few more things before I commit this perfect murder.*

Jack was ready to move on with his plan by the time Maria returned from Salsa's bedroom.

"Salsa is sleeping. I gave her some meds that will put her out for about two hours. I'll come back and check on her after we complete our next steps," Maria informed Jack. "Now, what is your plan, Jack? How are we going to make Diego pay?"

During the next hour, Maria and Jack put together their perfect murder plan.

The meeting with Diego was set at 4:00 p.m. in the parking lot of the restaurant at Seven Mile Bridge. Jack and Maria arrived at 3:00 p.m. to survey the parking lot and look for any cameras or surveillance devices in the area. Diego arrived at 3:50 p.m., accompanied by his two bodyguards.

Maria stepped out of the car, making sure all the men glimpsed her short, short skirt. *She is very good at distracting men*, Jack told himself. All of them watched Maria's approach.

"Diego. How are you?" Maria asked.

"*Excellente mi amor.*" Diego replied. "Where is your new friend…ah, Mr. Kennedy?"

"He is coming shortly. In the meantime, can I entertain your friends?" Maria asked.

"Sure," Diego replied. He watched as Maria took both his men into the bar.

Diego sat in his car and waited. He didn't have to wait long, because Jack appeared, pointing a gun at Diego's head from the backseat of his car.

"What the…" Diego began.

"Shut up. Move over and start the car," ordered Jack.

Diego began to move very slowly while Jack pressed the gun to his ear.

"Move very, very slowly, Diego," he said. "Anything you do from now on will be what I tell you, got it?"

Yes," Diego said.

"Now start the car and leave the parking lot. Get onto the highway, turn right, and follow my instructions exactly," Jack ordered.

Jack made Diego drive to an old abandon shipyard near Boot Key Harbor on the southern side of Marathon Key. There, Jack told Diego to turn around and then he shot him in the face and groin. There was no gunshot sound because Maria had given Jack a silencer for the .45 caliber pistol. Diego lay slumped in the driver's seat. Jack looked around and saw no one in the area. He stepped out of the vehicle and stopped again to listen and look.

Great, Jack thought, *now I need to prepare Diego for dinner. Dinner for the sharks, turtles, and crabs in the area.*

Five minutes later, Maria arrived. "Where is that S.O.–"

"He's about to sleep with the fish," Jack interrupted. "Did you bring the frozen bait blocks with you?"

"Of course. There are three of them in my trunk, Maria

replied. "Did you make that scum suffer?"

"Take a look at his body before he becomes fish bait," said Jack.

"Nice shot in his groin," said Maria.

"We need to wait about four hours until we can take him to the mangrove trees by the Vaca Cut Bridge."

"Why are we waiting? The chum will thaw, and it'll be no good."

"Listen, we need to bury this body where no cops will find him." explained Jack. "That means we wait and put him into the mangrove trees by Vaca Cut. Two days in the water with our chum and our anchor, and Diego will be a skeleton. Let's get him into the back seat. Be careful. I don't want any of his blood or clothing touching you."

Jack and Maria took the three bait blocks and put them into three insulated grocery bags. They covered his body with a blanket they found in the trunk of Diego's car.

By 9:00 p.m., they parked Diego's parked along a secluded road adjacent to the Vaca Cut Bridge. Wasting no time, Jack, in his wet suit and with his snorkel equipment, exited the car and quickly looked around. He was relieved to see no one was around.

He quickly took Diego's body out of the car and dragged it down to the edge of the water. Next, he fit the chum boxes against Diego's body, using Diego's clothing to keep the chum tight against his body. Then, he quickly got an old boat anchor and some nylon rope. He attached the rope around Diego's ankles and dragged him into the water. He slowly adjusted the body and the anchor line into the mangrove trees. When he was about twenty feet from the shore, he headed east, just along the mangrove trees growing in the area. He swam until he reached a break in the trees and then dropped the anchor in twenty-five feet of water. Then, he took Diego's body and dove under the tree roots. He slowly shoved Diego's body into several large holes in the root system of these trees. He came up for air and checked again to see if anyone was there. He then dragged the anchor along the bottom until he was under another group of roots. He took the diving knife and sliced the chum boxes open. He then resurfaced. He turned and took one last look at the body. To his surprise, a large crab was eating away at the chum at Diego's groin.

Sleep tight, you scumbag, Jacks thought. He came up to surface and checked again to see if the coast was clear. He headed to the car and left the area.

Now it was time to destroy Diego's car. Jack and Maria had already given this some thought. Maria had a good friend who got rid of problems like a stolen car, bloodstains, and possible fingerprints.

Maria met Jack at her friend's garage. An older man appeared.

"Maria, my friend. Is this the problem we discussed earlier today?" he asked, looking at Diego's car.

"Yes, my good friend," Maria replied.

"No problem, I will make it disappear now," said the

old man.

Ten minutes later, Maria and Jack were in Maria's penthouse.

"What did you do with Diego's two bodyguards?" Jack asked.

"They too are sleeping with the fish," Maria replied.

"How did you…" Jack stopped mid-question. "I don't want to know. Anyway, now can we change these clothes?"

Chapter Eight: Follow-Up Results—Day 1

August 19, 2021

I started looking into Jack Kennedy's background. Using the NCIC, CCH, and the DPS results, I recontacted each of the five departments in Florida mentioned in the DPS reports. Unfortunately, all the detectives who had worked any cases with Jack Kennedy named as a possible person of interest had retired and subsequently passed away. My first contact was Detective Easter at the Key West P.D.

"Hello, Detective Easter?" I asked.

"Yes?"

"Hi again. This is Detective Katie Hood calling from the Mangrove Sheriff's Department in Key Marathon," I stated. "Is this a good time to discuss a cold case file with you?"

"Sure, Detective. How can I help you?" Easter replied.

"I am working a homicide case involving a person who

has been identified as Mr. Jack Kennedy, male, Caucasian, born August 9, 1960. According to a DPS report, this Mr. Kennedy was identified as a possible suspect in a homicide case that occurred in your city in 1985. Could you give me any information on that case now?"

"I located the case file on this homicide a few hours ago," Easter replied. "Our homicide file indicates that the victim was identified as Bobby Jones, male, Caucasian, about twenty-one years old. Victim was a known drug dealer and employed several women who worked as prostitutes and sold drugs. Victim was found buried under several mangrove trees along the east side of the island. The autopsy revealed the victim was drowned, and there were several frozen bait boxes attached to his body. Our follow-up investigations identified three possible suspects, all involved in the drug industry, and all had several run ins with the victim one or two days before the body was found. All three suspects were identified over the next month; two were located, interrogated, and cleared. The third suspect was identified by one of the prostitutes as Jack Kennedy. The detective working the case at this time noted that this suspect had left the country and was believed to be in the Gulf working on a salvage ship looking for sunken treasures. At that time, the detective stated he had attempted to confirm that this individual was actually working on this salvage ship but had no luck. Additional attempts to locate this suspect ended after twelve months of searching the docks and ship records in the Key West. That's all we have on this homicide case."

"Interesting," I stated. "Could you please fax a copy of this report to me?"

"Sure, is there anything else I can assist you with, Detective Hood?" he asked.

"Did the detective working the case make any notations on how the body was found, or was the autopsy report available?"

"Interestingly, there was a one-page autopsy report done that listed drowning as the cause of death."

"Could you also fax that report to me?"

"Sure. Anything else?"

"Could you check your records for any other types of crimes where the suspect may have been identified as Jack Kennedy over the past thirty years or so? Then call me if you have any other crime reports involving this suspect."

"Sure, let me get back to you in a week if I find anything, OK?"

"Yes, thank you for your time and this follow-up information." I hung up the phone.

One down and four more to go. I then contacted four other police departments. In the conversations I had with detectives from the other police agencies, I found none of their old cold case files had been digitized. That meant I would have to wait a few more days to see if these detectives could locate any crime reports listing a Jack Kennedy as a possible suspect.

I was finally done for the day when I got a phone call from dispatch.

"Hood?" the dispatcher asked.

"Yes," I replied.

"One of our patrol officers just got a call about a possible body buried in the mangrove trees adjacent to the Vaca Cut Bridge. Can you respond?" she asked.

"Sure, can you also send Sgt. Doaks to assist me on this one?"

"Yes," the dispatcher stated before hanging up.

At 5:30 p.m., I got out of my car and stepped into a blast oven. The temperature was about 92 degrees, and the humidity was 98 percent. I had instant fog on my sunglasses, and my clothing immediately stuck to the sweat forming on my body.

"Crud," I said. "I hate this time of the year in Florida." I approached the deputy's vehicle and saw Deputy Jaca standing by.

"What have you got here?" I asked.

"I am not 100 percent sure, but I have two individuals who think they saw a body in the mangrove trees down this path."

"OK," I stated, "have you interviewed them yet?"

"No, I wanted to have a homicide detective here prior to the interview," he replied.

"OK," I stated, "let's talk to them and see what we may have." I began walking toward the witnesses, Fred and Joe, two older Caucasian men who were looking anxiously at me.

"Hello," I stated. I flashed my badge and introduced myself. "Detective Hood."

One of the men starting giggling. "Dang, I didn't know such a pretty woman was a cop, let alone a detective," he said.

"Yeah, well, I left my husband and baby at home," I said. "Now let's quit the crap and tell me what you were doing when you found this so-called body."

The man then got serious and told me that he and his buddy had come here around 4:30 p.m. to go fishing after work. They had just unpacked their poles, bait, and buckets, when Joe called Fred over to take a look at something. He began pointing in the water under one of the mangrove trees. There in the water appeared to be a ball of crabs feeding at something.

"I've been fishing in these waters for twenty years and never saw a bunch of crabs feeding like this," Joe declared.

"What makes you think there is a body under those crabs?" I asked Fred.

"Well, ma'am, I have seen this before," Fred stated. "I used to work at a pig farm in Siesta Key a few years ago. I saw what a bunch of crabs could do to a pig that fell into the ocean and drowned. The pig was caught under a bunch of mangrove tree roots, and the ball of crabs eating the pig looked just like what I saw here today."

"Thanks," I said. "Do you mind if I ask you some more questions?"

"No, ask me anything."

For the next five minutes, I asked Fred to retrace his steps from the car. I also asked him whether he or Joe saw any people, cars, or boats in the area when they arrived. Both said no to both questions.

I then directed Deputy Jaca to take both witnesses to his vehicle to get a statement. I also asked Deputy Jaca to check if either had been drinking prior arriving here.

I took out my cell phone and photographed the area, their vehicle, and their footsteps down to the beach. I also took several pictures of this ball of crabs in the area. I then turned my attention to the mangrove trees. I, too, was amazed to see this number of crabs.

What are they eating? I wondered.

Fifteen minutes later, Sgt. Doaks arrived at the scene.

"What do you have, Hood?" he asked.

"Not sure, Sarge," I responded. "If you look over there, you'll see a ball of crabs. Have you ever seen that many crabs in one place?"

Doaks looked at the mass of crabs.

"Sh –!"

"What? I asked. "What are you thinking?"

"Well rookie, this isn't my first rodeo with these crabs," Doaks croaked. "This is going to be a long, long night." He swore some more.

"What's going on?" I asked.

"This is the third time I've seen these types of crabs in

action, and in the other two cases, there was a body under that mass of crabs."

Doaks then looked at me. "We need to get a dive team here, we need to contact the on-duty shift commander, and then we need more men here to secure the scene," he said.

Crud. Another body, I thought. *How the heck are we going to get these crabs off whatever is under them?*

Doaks was right. It was a long night. The dive team arrived and began the task of getting the crabs off the body and then getting the body out of the water. Once the crabs were gone, they brought the body onto the shoreline.

Well, I think it's a body, or what's left of a body, I thought. The body appeared to be male, but there were no fingers, toes, eyes, or organs—only some parts of legs or arms. The body has been stripped of all flesh by the crabs.

"Hood, let's get to work. Do your job!" Doaks barked at me.

I started my preliminary investigations—pictures, evidence collection, etc. As I began my initial investigation, I asked one of the divers to go back into the water to check for any jewelry that may have dropped in the area. I also asked our boat patrol to look around the nearby area to see if there were any types of bait boxes caught in the roots or any other things that could be considered evidence.

I was still processing the scene when one of the divers came over to me and said, "I found this under the anchor holding the body in place."

He handed me a small wrist bracelet with the name Diego carved into it.

Interesting, I thought, *I wonder how many Diegos we have in the Keys.*

Dr. Spock arrived fifteen minutes later. What do you have, Hood?" he asked.

"Well, Doc, I think we have a male body, but I'm not sure of anything else," I told him.

"Interesting," he said. "I have seen six of these bodies before, and I still get queasy looking at the destruction crabs can do on a human body. Did you find any other piece of evidence at the scene or in the area?"

"We did find a small bracelet. I just put into our evidence bag. Would you like to see it?" I asked.

"No, thanks," he said. He then proceeded to put the body in a bag and exited the scene.

Doaks came back ten minutes later. "Hood, are you done yet?" he asked.

"No, I'm still processing the crime scene," I replied. "What have you been doing all this time?"

Doaks told me he was checking with the dive team to have them reenter the scene. He wanted them to look around a one-hundred-foot radius from the anchor site to see if there was any evidence. Doaks said the team had found nothing.

"What about shoes, a belt, a wallet, or a wristwatch?" I asked.

"Good questions, rookie, but these guys have been

through this before, and they know what to look for."

With that, Doaks left me and went back to the dive team supervisor.

Crud, I thought, *this has already been a long day, and I have a ton of paperwork still left to do.*

"Wrap it up rookie, I am hungry, and Rosie's has a breakfast special for biscuits and gravy right now," Doaks barked at me.

Two minutes later, we left together in my car. *Just one more day feeding Doaks*, I thought.

The next morning, I rolled over. *Crud, it can't be 6:00 a.m. yet.* I turned off my alarm clock and began some stretching exercises. After fifteen minutes of stretching, I got up and put my coffee pot on. Fifteen minutes later, I was in the car driving to work.

What am I going to find about these homicides today? I thought.

I got to my desk at 7:45 a.m. and began working on those blankets each baby was wrapped in.

Doaks arrived at my desk at 8:00 a.m. "Hood, what do you have planned today?" he asked.

"I was going to work on those blankets the two babies were wrapped in," I told him.

"No, we need to get over to Spock's office in twenty minutes. He's doing an autopsy on the body we found yesterday. Let's go!"

Twenty minutes later, we were in the autopsy room as

Dr. Spock conducted his preliminary exam on the body.

"No need for any incisions on this one; there is nothing left," Spock recorded into his machine. After looking over the body, Dr. Spock noticed a bullet hole in the forehead of the skeleton. Unfortunately, there were no shell fragments. The bullet went straight through the forehead and out the skull. He then looked at the ribs, vertebrae, and femur. Here, he found what appeared to be one knife wound on the right side of the body.

"Interesting," he told us, "it appears our victim was involved in a knife fight about ten years ago judging by the calcium on this rib."

I made a note in my cellphone to check if there were any aggravated assaults involving a knife wound reported to our local hospital about ten years ago. I also wanted to check our crime reports to see if our department investigated a knifing incident or aggravated assault during this projected period.

Dr. Spock then attempted to gather some samples of skin and bone samples for DNA results. He completed the autopsy in one hour.

"I will send these tissue samples to DPS crime lab this afternoon," he told us.

Great, I thought. *How long will these results take?*

"Anything else I can help you with now?" he asked.

"No," Doaks stated.

"Did you find anything else in the body bag or in the victim's skin?" I asked Dr. Spock.

"No, not at this time," Spock replied. "But I will have my techs go over the body bag again."

"Thanks," I told Spock.

Doaks headed out the door, yelling at me to come along. He needed to stop at McDonald's. True to form, I would have to pay again for his coffee.

At 1:30 p.m., I restarted my investigation into the two blankets both babies were wrapped in. I first Googled blanket patterns and found that there are several web sources on patterns and types of weaving materials. Next, I reviewed the pictures we had taken on both blankets, noting the patterns on both blankets looked like a southwestern pattern. I located a pattern source website called Ravelry.com, which had a wealth of information on blanket patterns. While looking at the different blanket patterns, I found a design similar to the designs on the baby blankets. The pattern was a handmade traditional Mexican yoga. Given this new information, I located a phone number at this website and made a call.

"Hello, Ms. Hill?" I asked.

"Yes," a woman answered.

"Hi, my name is Katie Hood, I am a homicide investigator in Mangrove County Sheriff's Department in Marathon Key," I told her. "I was wondering if I could talk to you to see if you could help me understand the blanket patterns listed in your website."

"Sure," the woman replied. "Can you tell me specifically what kind of information you need?"

"Well, I am not sure," I stated, "perhaps you can educate me on what types of weaving materials you have. Can you tell me anything about those blanket patterns?"

"Absolutely," Ms. Hill said. "First, is it possible for you to send me a picture of the blankets you mentioned?"

Yes," I replied, "can you give me your cellphone number?"

Within seconds, I sent the pictures to her.

"Wow," she exclaimed. "These patterns are very old. I would guess they are about fifty to a hundred years old. Can you take some close-up pictures of these patterns on each of the blankets focusing on the weave in the blanket?"

"Sure," I said. I sent them over.

"Well," Ms. Hill stated, "this pattern is very old and very distinctive."

"Can you elaborate more on this?" I asked her.

"Yes, but could you give me a few hours?" she asked. "I need to check a few weaving books."

"Of course," I said and then hung up.

Dr. Spock called me fifteen minutes later with some interesting news. "Hood?"

"Yes."

"You will not believe this, but I found a bullet slug in the body bag!" Spock exclaimed.

"What?" I shouted.

"Yes," he said, "my techs found a slug in the bottom of the body bag. It has to be a degree of luck."

"How do you think you missed it, and how did it get

there?"

"Listen Hood," Spock said angrily. "I believed we had thoroughly checked the body bag when the corpse arrived here, but I was wrong. Don't piss me off."

"Yes sir," I apologized and then kept my mouth shut!

"I am not sure, but perhaps when we lifted the body out of the bag, the bullet may have come out of the skin attached to his buttocks," Spock explained.

"That's interesting," I stated.

"Anyway," Spock continued, "I need you to come over here and seize this new evidence."

"Sure, I can be there in twenty minutes."

I arrived at Dr. Spock's office twenty minutes later. While I waited for him, I thought about where that bullet could have come from.

"Listen, Hood, "Dr. Spock said by way of greeting. "I think I know where that bullet was located and why we were so lucky in recovering it. I went back over the autopsy pictures again, and I think I know why we have this bullet slug. I believe our victim may have been shot in the groin area, which would explain a slight mark I found on his right hipbone. I believe the bullet lodged in the muscle tissue in the buttocks which was not eaten by the crabs. I think that getting the body into the bag, lifting it into the morgue wagon, and then the shifting during the drive from the crime scene back to the office may have sloughed off enough skin to let the bullet fall out."

"Interesting find," I told him.

"Yes, we are very lucky the crabs didn't eat this part of the body and that the bullet remained in place until we put the body into the freezer," he exclaimed.

"Thanks," I stated. "Anything else?"

"No," he said, "but please let me know what you get when running the bullet through the National Integrated Ballistic Identification Network (NIBIN) striation pattern database."

"OK," I said and left his office.

At 1:00 p.m., Doaks came into my office holding a coffee cup and a doughnut.

"Hood, where are we on those follow-up reports on the information given in the NCIC and DPS reports?" he asked.

"Glad you asked," I replied. "I did some research on the two blankets we found wrapped around our baby victims. There is a website called—"

"Wait one second," Doaks yelled, "why are you going to a website?"

"Because I found there is a lot of information on blanket patterns and weavings on the internet if you just look!" I told him.

Doaks was taken back. "You found a website on the internet with information on blanket patterns and weavings?"

"Yes," I told him, "Welcome to the twenty-second century in forensics!"

Doaks then shut up then I told him what I had found.

"Yes," I said. "And more good news: Dr. Spock found

a bullet slug in the body bag of our latest murder victim."

"What the heck," Doaks sputtered. I told him Spock had guessed that the bullet was in the muscle hanging from the buttocks section of our victim.

"I took the bullet slug and placed it into evidence," I said. "I was going to have it shipped out to the FBI lab for a striation pattern data base for an analysis this afternoon."

"Great work, Hood," said Doaks. "I'm proud of you and the work you've done so far on this case. Now, let's get something to eat." Doaks motioned me to come along. I just sat in my chair and stared at him. *What just happened?* I asked myself, *did I just get a compliment from Doaks?* Then we left because Doaks was starving.

"Detective Hood?" she asked, it was Ms. Hill.

"Yes."

"I apologize for keeping you on hold for so long. I wanted to verify my findings on your two blankets. I want to give you the exact information I have researched."

"Great," I stated, "what did your research indicate?"

"First, you need to know that this pattern is very old and very distinctive. My research indicates it was first developed by the Creek Indians, later known as the Seminoles. The pattern was used very early in the 1770s and then was found again in Spain in the 1800s. There was a family name associated with this pattern in Spain—the Hernandez family located in the Seville area.

"The weave pattern on these two blankets is a very old

weaving form," she continued. "My guess is that these blankets are probably between thirty and a hundred years. Can you have a test done in your crime lab to determine the age of the weaving material?"

"Yes," I stated, "I can contact our DPS Crime Lab and have them look into getting that done."

"One other thing," Ms. Hill stated. "Do you have any old established families living in your area with the last name Hernandez?"

"I don't know, but I'll check on this as soon as we are done," I replied.

"Great," said Ms. Hill, "do you need any additional information?"

"Yes," I told her, "Could you please type a written statement addressed to me explaining all of your findings and provide me with a contact number and address in case I need more information in the future?"

"Of course."

Wow, I thought to myself, *a possible suspect name, and a possible lead on these two baby victims.*

This was at least a start. I was just about to call Doaks when he showed up at my office. "Hood," he asked, "what are you doing now?"

"Sgt. Doaks, please sit. I have some information on those blankets I need to share with you, and I have a question for you too," I told him.

Doaks sat down, looking anxiously at me.

I then briefed him on my findings and research Ms. Hill had done on the two blankets. Doaks jaw nearly dropped to the floor. "You got all of that information starting with the internet?" he asked.

"Yes sir, and I am willing to bet there is more information we will find after we send a sample of the weaving material to our DPS crime lab," I told him.

Doaks continued to look dumbfounded.

"Now, I have a question for you," I stated, "is there a family in our area by the last name of Hernandez?" I asked him.

"Hernandez? I will have to get back to you on this," Doaks said. He then left.

Interesting, I thought. *I wonder where he went and what he is doing.*

Then my phone rang. It was Officer Jaca.

"Detective Hood?"

Yes, what do have for me today?"

"Good news and bad news," he stated. "The good news is I now know why Mutt left the immediate area and sat down adjacent to the seawall. The bad news is Mutt's actions indicate there are one or more bodies buried near this seawall."

Crud, I thought. *Doaks will go nuts given this information.* "OK, thanks for getting back to me. Can you tell me when you and Mutt can come back here?" I asked.

"I don't know the answer to that question," Officer Jaca stated.

Officer Jaca then hung up.

"Crud, crud, crud!" I yelled out loud. "This is going to be a very long day!" I then left my office to search for Doaks.

Where the heck is he? I thought. Two minutes later, I located him coming out of the men's restroom.

"Doaks!" I shouted.

"Yeah, Hood. What now?" he asked.

"Let's go into your office," I suggested and headed toward his desk.

"All right, Hood. I am at my desk waiting patiently for your request," Doaks said, glaring at me.

"Well, we have another problem at the crime scene," I told him. "K-9 Officer Jaca called me five minutes ago and said that we probably have at least one more body buried by the seawall."

"What the heck are you talking about? One or more bodies buried at the crime scene at the Hut?" he asked.

"Remember after we found the three buried bodies? How Mutt moved over to the seawall and sat? I reminded Doaks.

Yes," he replied.

"Do you remember Jaca's reaction?" I asked him. "He said he'd never seen Mutt do that before and that he was going to research it."

"Yes, I do now," Doaks said.

"Well, we're going to have to go back to the Hut, get another cadaver dog, and dig up the area again," I told Doaks.

"This is not good. Not good for me, for you, or for the

department," Doaks croaked. "We'll look bad, like rookie detectives."

"Tough," I told him. "We need to get on this ASAP. We need to tell the sheriff now, get more manpower reassigned there, and get another cadaver dog down here as soon as possible."

OK," Doaks agreed, "let me talk to the chief deputy and the sheriff about this. In the meantime, please call your buddy Clutch."

"Sure," I told him.

I called Clutch at 4:00 p.m. and he was not overjoyed.

"Hood, what's going on now?" he asked.

"Clutch, I have a big problem here, and I need your help now," I told him.

"Um, this is really going to cost you," he said. "What do you have and what do you want now?"

I filled him on what Officer Jaca had told me about Mutt's behavior at the seawall.

"So now you need a cadaver dog," Clutch declared. "Anything else you think you may need, Hood?"

"Yes, there is," I replied. "I would like to try to get some ground penetrating radar equipment. And could you contact a friend of yours in the DPS Crime lab to see if they could put a rush order on the DNA samples we sent them last week of our two baby victims?"

"Sure, and would you like me to stop the six other major homicide investigations our department is dealing with and send these resources immediately to you?" Clutch asked sarcastically.

"Come on, Clutch," I pleaded, "we may have one or more bodies buried here. That could mean five or six victims. That's a huge priority for our department now. Can you help me, please?" I tried to sound as nice as possible.

"Hood, you are impossible. But let me see what I can do, given this latest information," he said. "Can I call you back in an hour?"

"Sure. Clutch, we'll have a nice dinner at my place once this investigation is done, OK?"

"Right, Hood," he said and then hung up.

Doaks came flying into my office five minutes later.

"Hood, let's go," he ordered. "The sheriff and the chief deputy want to speak us right now!"

Doaks was actually running down the hall. He turned back to me and said, "Hood, move your hind parts now!"

Interesting opportunity to see your sheriff and the chief deputy under these conditions. I thought Doaks would go into cardiac arrest by the time we reached the reception area for the sheriff.

Once we arrived, Doaks told the sheriff's secretary to please wait a minute so he could use the restroom.

Five minutes later, Doaks, looking a lot better, told the secretary to let the sheriff know we were here. Sheriff Jones and Chief Deputy Smith met us at the door. "Sgt. Doaks and Detective Hood, glad you made time to meet with us on homicide case. Please come in," the sheriff stated.

For the next hour and a half, I told these men the entire investigation process we had carried out, the follow-up information to date, and the request I put into Clutch for additional equipment. Both men looked at me then at each other for a few minutes.

"Do you have anything to add to Hood's report?" the sheriff then asked Doaks.

"Ah, no sir, she has done an excellent job," he stated.

Again, there were several minutes of silence.

"Joe, we are going to need $50,000 more in our overtime budget to handle this case now. Where can we find this kind of money?" Chief Deputy Smith ask the sheriff.

The sheriff looked at his computer, then at us, and then called his secretary into his office. "Jane, I need you to look at our salary savings over the past six months. I believe we have about $70,000 in unexpended salary savings that we'll need to transfer into our overtime budget. Can you verify my figures and let me know after we are done with our discussion here?"

"Yes sir," Jane said and then left.

Then the sheriff looked at me then said, "Hood, Sgt. Doaks is tied up on a special investigation for me and will not be able to help you for the next two days. Can you run this case by yourself until he's done?"

"Yes sir," I replied. "Thank you for this opportunity."

"Good," the Sheriff stated. He then got up and the

rest of us followed suit. After a few handshakes, I left, while Doaks stayed in the sheriff's office.

This is my chance, I thought, *now I can run this homicide case using all the forensic resources I can get!*

Chapter Nine: Follow-Up Reports—Day 2

August 21, 2021

At 5:00 a.m., I was up and planning the next steps in this investigation. I created a list of things to get done:

Get a K-9 or a ground penetrating radar at the original crime scene;

Research the name Hernandez living in the Keys over the past fifty to a hundred years;

Follow up with the cold case sections from the other four police departments;

Ask the Sheriff for additional money to process the DNA on the two babies;

Contact a botanist and see if there are any leads from the evidence found with the body in the mangrove trees.

I left at 6:00 a.m., coffee in hand, and headed for the sheriff's department. At 7:00 a.m., I got a call from Clutch.

"Hood?"

"Yes, Clutch. What news do you have for me?"

"Well, I cannot shake anything loose as far as any K-9 units available until next week," he said. "However, I did locate a ground radar penetrating unit in the Cocoa Beach Police Department you can use. It should be there by Friday."

"OK, great. Does this unit come with an operator or am I supposed to learn how to use it in the next twenty-four hours?" I asked.

"Hood, your attitude is beginning to piss...me off," Clutch said. "Just accept what I can give you, OK?"

"Sorry, Clutch," I said. "I've just been put in charge of this investigation, and I have a lot of leads I need to start and a lot of territory to cover."

"Accepted on one condition," he said.

"OK, what?" I asked.

"You need to get the Chief in Cocoa Beach a bottle of his favorite gin, Tanqueray No. 10. OK?"

"Sure," I replied. I knew that sometimes in police work, these little rewards went a long way in creating friendships and borrowing equipment from one department to another.

"I'll have it shipped to him today," I told Clutch.

"OK then, I'll talk to you later." Clutch hung up.

At 8:30 a.m., Doaks came over to my office. "What do you have going today?"

"Not sure but I am working on a list of six things," I told him. "I just heard from Clutch at the DPS crime lab;

he may be able to get us a ground radar penetrating unit here by Friday."

"Great. Does that come with an operator or is this something you'll learn from the internet?" Doaks chortled.

"No sir, the ground unit comes with an operator from Cocoa Beach Police Department," I told him. "Hey, did you have any luck finding a Hernandez family living in the Keys over the past fifty to a hundred years?"

"Crap," he stated. "I forgot about that. Shall we go to McDonald's for coffee while I think about it?"

"No Doaks, I don't have time for that. I need to follow up on one critical request about money, and I need your advice on it," I said.

OK, how can I help you this time?" he asked.

"I want to ask the Sheriff for $1500 to have a private lab process the DNA of the two babies we found last week," I told him.

"$1500. Is that all?" Doaks asked.

"Yes, I did some research and found three private labs in the Keys that will complete the DNA analysis, and all of them are certified by Dr. Spock and the courts in the Keys," I told him.

"OK, "he stated. "Let me think for a minute or two about this and get back to you."

Great, I thought to myself. *Doaks getting back to me will take hours, if not days, if he gets sidetracked*. I looked at my watch.

By 9:30 a.m., the number of leads in this investigation had begun to double. I received a call from Detective Carter from Florida City P.D. He told me that he had identified a person of interest named Jack Kennedy in his cold case files who was wanted in connection to two embezzlement cases in 1992.

He filled me in on the details of the cases. "The suspect, Mr. Jack Kennedy, was involved with two widows on two separate occasions. He told them he needed some startup money to find a sunken treasure ship about nine miles off Key Marathon. He had both women sign contracts, giving him their money to buy a fully equipped salvage boat. After both women had given him $500,000 apiece, both had second thoughts. They recontacted Jack Kennedy at the phone number he had given them, but it was disconnected. Then both women visited the residence he had listed on their contracts. It was an abandoned garage. Both arrived at the same place at the same time and begun to share their stories. They reported him to the police. The detective working this case attempted to locate Mr. Kennedy over the next twelve months, but he was never located."

"Do you have any other information on this suspect?" I asked.

"Not really," said Detective Carter. "The report just indicated that both women had an ongoing affair with him during this time frame. Both did not know any personal information about him except his phone number and address."

"OK, is there any information on an approximate age, height, weight, or other physical characteristics?" I asked.

"No, they could not give the detective any specific information, except the report states that they both had a smile on their face when asked about his physical characteristics," he replied.

"Thanks for the follow up. Can you fax a copy of your department's case report to me?" I asked.

"Sure, I'll fax it to you in about five minutes." Then Detective Carter hung up.

"Crud, crud, crud," I muttered. Nothing specific about Jack Kennedy except he had about $1 million to play with before disappearing in 1992. "I hope the other departments have some more specific information," I said out loud.

Five minutes later, I had three phone calls, one from Naples Police Department, one from Agent Smith with the IRS, and one from a DPS Financial Investigator Sgt. Rock. I let two of the three calls go to voicemail, and I picked up the Naples Police Department's call.

"Hello," I said, "this is Detective Hood speaking."

"Good morning, my name is Sgt. Wendell. I am following up on your inquiry about a male named Jack Kennedy," he said.

"Great. What kind of information does your department have on this individual?" I asked.

"Well, we have a Jack Kennedy listed as a possible homicide suspect in two cases occurring in 1995," he replied.

"Two homicide cases?" I asked.

"Yes, a white male named Jack Kennedy was listed as a primary suspect in two drug-related homicides in 1995," he continued.

"Do you have time to go over each of these cases now?" I asked.

"Sure," he said.

For the next hour, Sgt. Wendell went over the backgrounds of both cases with me. Both involved drugs, prostitutes, and lots of money ranging between $350,000 and $800,000. In one of the cases, a male whose name was Jack Kennedy was the last person seen leaving the area with the homicide victim. The woman witnessed this event said she had slept with Jack the night before and managed to take a one hundred bill out of his wallet while he was sleeping. She also told the detective she saw a Florida driver's license and memorized his information. The woman gave this information to the detective assigned to this homicide.

"The next case is about the same," Wendell continued, "same crime, same witnesses, same prostitutes who slept with Jack and saw him leaving the area with the homicide victim."

"Did the detective on this case give any additional information on his follow-up actions?" I asked.

"Very little information was found in the follow-up report," Wendell explained. "The detectives assigned to both cases combined their resources and tried to locate Mr. Kennedy. But he was never seen in the area again."

"Can you fax me a copy of both reports and any follow-up information or autopsy report?" I asked.

"Sure. Oh, one thing about both autopsy reports," Wendell said. "Both bodies were left under water, stuck into the root system of some mangrove trees, and eaten away by the crabs in the area. There was not much evidence found at the crime scene."

"Interesting," I said, "our department is dealing with a recent homicide where the victim was found stuck under some mangrove roots, and crabs had eaten most of his body too."

I had one more question for him. "Did you find any evidence around the bodies in either case?"

"Not initially, but twenty-four hours after one body was found, one of our detectives found two cardboard bait box containers stuck in one of the mangrove trees about twenty feet from the burial site," he said.

"Did you have any luck finding any evidence on the boxes or in the water below the body?" I asked.

"No, unfortunately," he replied.

I thanked him and hung up. Interesting how these homicide victims were buried in a similar fashion. I needed to find more information on my recent homicide scene. I then phoned dispatch.

"Sarah?" I asked.

"Yes," she replied.

"I need you to send two deputies to meet me at Vaca Cut Bridge."

"OK detective, I will dispatch two deputies now."

I was heading out the door when Doaks yelled at me, "Hood, where are you going in such a hurry?"

"Doaks, I just found another connection to our recent homicide in the mangrove roots," I replied.

"What?" Doaks asked.

"Naples P.D. had two homicides cases in 1995. Both victims were found buried under mangrove trees with most of their bodies eaten by crabs. In both cases, there were cardboard bait boxes found in the area. I am heading back to Vaca Cut with two other deputies to search the area one more time looking for possible evidence."

Doaks grabbed my shoulder on my way out. "Wait a second, I have good news for you," he said. "I talked to the Chief Deputy about getting some money to fund the cost of a private DNA analysis. He said sure, just contact his secretary with the lab's name, address, and billing information."

"Great. Can you do that now?" I asked.

Doaks was not expecting that question, but I needed the help. "Please help me with this," I asked. Then I was gone.

At 10:30 a.m., I stepped into another blast furnace. The temperature was 95 degrees and the humidity was 99 percent. My sunglasses immediately fogged up. *Yuck, I hate this time of year in Florida,* I thought. I headed down to the latest crime scene and look over the entire scene again. Two minutes later, I was approached by two deputies.

"Detective Hood?" they asked.

"Yes," I told them, "thanks for getting here so soon."

For the next few minutes, I brief them on what I was looking for and how they could help me find more evidence. Both deputies took off. Fifteen minutes later, both came back saying they saw nothing.

"Thanks," I told them, leaving the scene.

As I was waiting by the water's edge, a boat approached me. "Can I help you?"

"Sure," I stated, and the boat stopped on the shore. "Hi," I told the driver. "My name is Detective Katie Hood."

"Yes, I know who you are. I am your neighbor across the canal from your parents' place. My name is Keith. How I help you?"

"Can you help me do a little exploring in this area?" I asked him.

"Sure," he replied. We began to slowly follow the mangrove tree line. I ask him to look for any type of materials or boxes floating in the area. We cruised up the tree line for about fifty feet when I asked him to stop. I spotted something white behind a large mangrove tree about fifteen feet in front of us.

"Can you get your boat any closer?" I asked.

"Not sure," Keith replied, "I am worried about the prop getting stuck."

"Could you lift the prop out of the water and let me row the boat a little closer?"

"OK."

As we got closer, I saw a floating white cardboard box.

"Can you hold onto this tree branch for a second while I try to get that box attached to the tree root?" I asked Keith.

"Sure," he said, "be careful. I've seen a lot of strange animals in these trees."

Great, I thought, *strange animals in the trees?* I stepped out onto the roots of the closest tree. Once on them, I realized that my shoes were soaking wet and there were about a hundred little fleas, crabs, and flies attacking me.

Keep going, I told myself. I reached the tree and found a white cardboard bait box stuck there. I pulled it out using my gloved right hand and put it onto an evidence bag.

As I was heading back, I saw something just under the surface of the water. The object appeared to be shiny, and it was stuck on top of one of the mangrove roots. I reached for it and fell into the bay.

Great, I thought, *I'll now be eaten by sharks, crabs, or other fish*. I floated in the water, trying to reach the shiny object. Keith saw what was going on and threw me a grappling hook. I grabbed it and reached the object. To my surprise, a belt was attached to it. I pulled it toward me while treading water. Keith rowed over to my location and pulled me onboard. I then glanced in the water. A giant crab had followed the belt up to the boat.

Thank you, Lord, I thought. *I would not like to be bitten by that crab.*

Keith looked at me with a funny expression. "Do you always fall into the ocean while trying to find evidence?" he asked, throwing a towel at me.

"Yes, this is not the first time and probably won't be the last," I told him. "Thanks for your help. Can you take me back to the shore? I need to get these things back to the evidence locker."

"Sure," he said. He dropped me off, waved goodbye, and headed toward the Gulf of Mexico. I got to my car, marked the belt as evidence, then put it into another evidence bag. I glanced one more time at the bait container. Under the front flap was a sticker marked Captain Hooks Bait Shop.

Great, now I can go to Captain Hooks Bait shop across the bridge and see if I can find more information, I thought. I started my car and realized I'd probably wrecked another pair of shoes and perhaps my cuffs and my gun. Everything was soaked in salt water and had to be cleaned as soon as possible. I headed to the Captain Hooks Bait Shop.

Captain Hooks Bait Shop was located on the Vaca Cut, a waterway between the Atlantic Ocean and the Gulf of Mexico. The bait shop had been there for fifty years. Everything needed by a saltwater fisherman, or diver, or boat driver was here. The shop was crammed with equipment for fishing, all sorts of baits, hooks, and other diving gear. It also had a variety of fishing bait.

I asked one of the clerks, Mary, if she could help me. "Sure, Katie, is it?" she asked.

"Yes, "I replied. I have been coming to this bait shop for the past thirty years with my dad.

"Listen Mary, I need your help," I told her. "Please look at this box. Do you recognize it?"

"Yes, I do," she replied, "that's one of our bait boxes. We sell about a hundred of these each day."

"Great, do you have video camera recording customers buying this type of bait over the past week or so?" I asked.

"I think so," she said. She took me back to an office with a screen showing the security camera feed. "I need to check with the boss about letting you see the recordings," she said.

Mary left the office to find her boss, Captain Hook. Captain Hook is the son of the original owner of the bait shop. He grew up in this bait shop and knows a lot about fishing and diving. Captain Hook showed up about three minutes later.

"Hello, Katie, is it?" he asked.

"Hi. Yes, I am Katie," I replied. I explained why I was there and the importance of trying to locate a possible suspect in the homicide I was investigating.

"Is it possible for me to look at your videos showing all the transactions occurring in the past week?" I asked.

"Not sure," he replied, "but I will check with my computer company and see how we can arrange it. Can you wait about fifteen minutes?"

Sure," I said. I then waited. Waiting in soaking wet clothes is not a good experience. Especially when you are waiting in a very cold air-conditioned shop.

Finally, Captain Hook came back to me. "Katie, I think we can get the videos you need," he said. "But it may take another day while they copy all the video film over the past week."

"How long will it take them if you put a rush on this?" I asked. "I believe your video may provide our department with a picture of a suspect involved in a recent homicide."

"Really?" he asked, "let me see what I can do then to get this going faster."

Thirty minutes later, he came back with good news. "They can get you a copy of all the video over the past week."

"Great. Can they deliver their video stick to you here?" I asked.

"Video stick?"

"Yes, videos can be easily transferred onto a memory stick called a jump drive. You know, the little flat looking object you put into the side of a laptop?"

"So that's what those little things are called," he said. "OK, I'll call you when they deliver it."

I give him my cell number, thanked him for his help, and then left.

I radioed dispatch to tell them I was out of service for the hour. Just as I arrived at my apartment, Doaks called.

"Hood, why did you calling out of service for one hour?"

"Doaks, I have to change my clothes. I fell into the ocean, and I need to clean my gun and my handcuffs."

"You fell into the ocean?"

"Yes, I found some possible evidence about forty yards north of our crime scene. I gotta go."

Forty minutes later, I was back at work. I had changed into clean clothes and my gun and cuffs were thoroughly cleaned and oiled.

Doaks called me just as I was about to enter the station. "Hood, you won't believe what I found," he said. "There's been a Hernandez family living here in the Keys for the past fifty years or so."

"What did you find about this family?" I asked.

"Can you meet me at the McDonald's on your way in?" he asked.

"Sure," I replied, reaching for my wallet. I had ten bucks, enough to buy us both a cup of coffee.

"Great, I have a lot to tell you," he said and then hung up.

Doaks was sitting in McDonald's when I arrived. I couldn't believe my eyes. Doaks had bought himself a large coffee, and he had one waiting for me. *Am I dreaming?* I thought. I looked at the date on my cell phone. August 21, my lucky day. I punched the calendar app on my phone and left a star. This was a day to remember.

"Sit down, Hood," he ordered. "Look I bought you coffee. Nice, huh?"

"Cut the crap," I replied, sitting down across him. "This better be good."

Doaks then filled me in. He told me that the name

Hernandez sounded very familiar, but he could not remember why. He then realized he'd worked on a case during his early years as a homicide detective involving an embezzlement charge against Jose Hernandez and his wife Maria. The case involved Jose embezzling several million dollars from his parents' restaurant, called the Hut.

"The Hut?" I asked. "That restaurant in Point Key?"

"Yes, that restaurant," Doaks stated. He continued to tell me about the case. "Jose Hernandez plea bargained out of a major felony and served ten years in prison. He got out after four years based on his good behavior. His wife Maria was never charged. Jose's parents were one of original founding families of Key Marathon. They settled here in the late 1890s and built the original Hut, then called the Hacienda, in 1920. After the Okeechobee Hurricane destroyed most of the homes in Marathon in 1928, the Hernandez family bought more property adjacent to the Hacienda location and rebuilt the restaurant, renaming it the Hut.

"I found the original report and the follow up-reports on this case," Doaks continued. "It appears Jose had inherited a lot of money from one of his uncles living in Seville, Spain. Maria found out, and she began to hide all the money. Initially, Jose did not find out about the offshore accounts because Maria controlled all the Hut's financial record. Later, Jose stumbled upon some receipts from these offshore banks that showed Maria's spending habits on drugs and other things. The follow-up investigations indicated that she was a suspect in the homicides of two drug dealers in the mid-1990s. Again, there was no conclusive evidence to convict her of anything. The conclusion on the follow up reports indicated that detectives located the source of Jose's inheritance as a family winery business. His family was also associated with a patent for a certain weave of blankets during the early 1880s. That concludes the report and my information."

I looked at him. He was beaming like a kid who had just won a prize.

"Thanks, Doaks," I said. I wondered if anyone had ever conducted an audit of the Hut's finances or checked the property records of the Hut, the original Hacienda, or the apartment complexes located adjacent it.

"What do you think about this information?" I asked Doaks.

"I think there is a lot more to this family if we begin to dig a little deeper," he said. "I need to do a little more digging into this case, and I need to check with some of my connections in the financial crimes unit in DPS."

"Good idea, and one more thing," I replied. "Doaks, I need you to follow up on some more financial information on our homicide victim, Jack Kennedy."

"Why Jack Kennedy?" he asked.

"I had two agents call me this morning, one from the IRS and one from the State of Florida, Financial Crimes Unit, wanting to talk to me about Jack Kennedy. I'm swamped following up on another possible lead on our homicide victim found in the mangrove trees yesterday. Can you help me?" I pleaded.

"OK rookie," he replied, "but this will cost you another lunch at Rosie's."

It was time to go. Doaks and I left McDonald's and headed back to work.

At 5:00 p.m., Captain Hook called me on my cell.

"Katie, I got that stick, jump drive, or whatever you called it, here on my desk. Can you come and get it?" he asked.

"Yes," I said, "I'll be right over." Fifteen minutes later, I picked up the video stick and returned to my computer.

Dang, it's 5:30 p.m. already. Another long night, I thought.

I began watching the video tape from the bait shop at 6:00 p.m. By 11:30 p.m., I was falling asleep. I saw no one on these tapes that looked like Jack Kennedy or anyone else associated with the homicide cases.

Tomorrow is another day, I thought. I headed home.

The next morning, I was back at my desk, looking at the videos from the bait shop.

Doaks came in and looked at me. "Any luck identifying any suspects in our homicide case?" he asked.

"Nothing. No one looks suspicious in these tapes," I replied.

"Well, I have some good news," he said. "I talked to my contacts in the financial crimes section in DPS today. They've been trying to get enough information to audit Maria Hernandez's businesses for the past year. In fact, they are working with the IRS to develop enough evidence to get a federal warrant on her to confiscate the Hut's financial records.

"Hey, do you know Maria Hernandez?" Doaks suddenly asked me.

"No, not really," I replied.

"Well, here's her picture. I thought if you saw her, you would remember her," he stated.

I look at her picture. She was a very attractive woman. Suddenly, something began to click in my brain.

"Can I have this?" I asked, waving the picture.

"Sure, keep it as long as you want." He left.

I looked at her picture one more time. She looked familiar. Where had I seen her?

I looked back at the videotapes, and then it hit me. I saw her buying bait at the bait store. I stopped the tape and set it back to ninety-six hours ago. I started at the beginning again. Four hours later, just as I was about to go give up, I saw her buying bait boxes at Captain Hooks.

There she was, at 10:30 a.m. on August 17, buying three bait boxes at the Captain Hoods bait shop. I stopped the video, noted the date, time, and location, and then ran to find Doaks.

"Doaks, Doaks, come with me now!"

He wasn't at his desk, so I went outside the men's room and waited. Five minutes later, Doaks came out of the room and jumped. "Hood do not scare me like that!" he yelled.

"Doaks, I think I found something on the videotapes

from Captain Hooks," I told him. "Let's go over to my office. I want you to see a possible suspect."

"OK," he said, following me.

I restarted the tape and let Doaks watch. "Well, crap. There she is buying three boxes of bait at Captain Hooks," Doaks exclaimed. "Why is she buying bait at this hour?"

"I don't know yet, but I believe we may have another lead on our recent homicide case," I said.

"You may have something here. What are you going to do next? he asked.

"I think I'm going to get that bait box in the evidence room. If I am lucky, I may be able to get a fingerprint off it, but I am not sure," I replied.

How can I get prints off this type of box? I thought. I went on the internet and began to research how to lift fingerprints from a wet surface. I found that it was possible using an SPR (small particle reagent) chemical mix, and I told Doaks about this option.

"Go get them, tiger," he said and then left.

I decided to call Clutch. "Listen, I need your help. I found some possible evidence on a wet cardboard bait box. If I let the cardboard box dry, could I take prints off it using the SPR method?"

"The SPR chemical spray has a great possibility to do that," he confirmed. "Let me know how it turns out."

I went to our department's property room. Well, it wasn't just a room, but several rooms, a garage, and some holding areas. I asked Sgt. Jones, where I could find the property I'd left in the locker this afternoon.

Five seconds later, he brought the evidence bag with the bait box. "Here you go, please sign the log, and you can have it," he instructed. I signed the log, took the evidence, and left. I went to our crime lab and took out the box. It appeared to be dry.

Interesting, I thought. *I fell into the ocean, so why is it dry?* Just then, I remembered I had put the box into an evidence bag I had on me before falling into the water. *Good save,* I told myself.

I put the opened box on a table and got the SPR spray. I said a quick prayer and then took the box in my gloved hands and looked at it under a magnifying glass. It looked like there were two prints on the lid. I was getting excited now. I carefully set the box down, sprayed it, and waited for a few seconds. Then it happened—two fingerprints appeared. I took our digital close-up property camera and carefully photographed each print. Then I transferred the camera prints into our AFIS (automatic fingerprint identification system) machine, a system used by all law enforcement agencies in the United States. It is a database of any person who has been fingerprinted by a governmental agency in the past fifty years.

Now it was time to wait. It could take twelve hours or longer. I looked at my clock; it was 8:30 p.m. Time to go home. I put the evidence bag back into the evidence locker and left for home.

Doaks called me at 7:00 a.m. the next morning, ordering me to get into headquarters ASAP. I looked at my clock and realized I'd overslept. I quickly got dressed and arrived at the station twenty minutes later.

"Good morning, Sgt. Doaks," I greeted him. "What's going on?"

"Hood," he said excitedly. "I just got a call from Jones in property. Your AFIS check came back with two hits, and you won't believe who these hits are."

"OK, who?" I asked.

"One print belongs to Jack Kennedy the other to Maria Hernandez."

"What?" I ask. "Maria Hernandez and Jack Kennedy!"

"Yes, Hood. Now we can really begin to look into the Kennedy homicide and our recent homicide in the ocean."

"What's your game plan?" I asked Doakes.

"I am thinking on this. Give me an hour and then we'll meet in my office, OK?"

"Sure," I said. I got some coffee, returned to my desk, and began to think. What was next in these homicide cases? Somehow, I had to get Jack Kennedy and Maria Hernandez in the same location or make a solid connection between these two to move forward on any warrants.

Doaks and I met in his office around 8:30 a.m.

Doaks asked me if I had any thoughts on the next step to take. I told him that I needed to find a connection between Jack Kennedy and Maria Hernandez. He liked that idea and told me he would work with the IRS and DPS financial crimes squad to try to get more information on Maria Hernandez and her financial records at the Hut. I went back to my desk and got copies of Jack Kennedy and Maria Hernandez's driver's license pictures. It was time for me to start making a connection between the two.

I decided to visit the Hut. One of the waitresses, Susan, recognized me and came over.

"Hi, Katie. How can I help you?" she asked. "I need to see if anyone here recognizes this man," I told her, holding up a picture of Jack.

"Come with me, I'll take you back into our kitchen, and you can show this picture to all our waitresses and cooks," she said, ushering me to the back. In the kitchen, I identified myself and passed out the picture.

After all of them had looked at the picture, one of the cooks, Juan, asked to speak with me alone. I thanked all the staff and took Juan into a private office. There he told me, in hushed whispers, that Mr. Kennedy had arrived here a few nights ago. He was dropped off at the Hut by Salsa, Ms. Hernandez's daughter. Juan told me that he had been instructed by Ms. Hernandez to take Mr. Kennedy over to the apartment complex next door and tell him to go to the fifth-floor penthouse to meet her.

"Are you sure this was the man?" I asked Juan.

"Yes," he confirmed.

I asked Juan if he could give me a written statement.

Juan hesitated. "I do not know how to write English," he said.

"That's OK," I told him, "I can get you a Spanish speaking officer." I called dispatch. Fifteen minutes later, Deputy Javiera arrived and took Juan's statement in Spanish. She then translated it and made a follow up-report.

Now, with some additional information, I returned to my desk and began checking the passenger logs of flights into the Key West Airport over the past ten days. I found Jack Kennedy's name on flight 2324 from Bermuda into Miami then onto Key West on August 13. I called the airlines and asked for a copy of the manifest, and it was faxed to me within an hour. I entered that into evidence.

I call Doaks to update him on my news. I also asked if he had any updates on the financial records involving Jack Kennedy and Maria Hernandez over the past decade.

"Nothing yet," he said and hung up.

I left the office and headed home. Time for a glass of wine.

Chapter Ten: Pieces Falling Into Place

August 23, 2021

At 7:00 a.m., I was putting together another plan of action involving Maria Hernandez and her relationship with Jack Kennedy. Doaks had informed me the financial squad in our state DPS was working with the IRS to obtain enough evidence to get a warrant on the Hut's financial statements.

As I was sipping my coffee, I got a call from the FBI headquarters at Quantico.

"Hello, Detective Hood speaking."

"Detective Hood, this is special ATF agent Gene Jones," said the voice on the other line. "I need to verify that you are Detective Katie Hood."

"OK," I agreed. "How are you going to do this?"

"You have just received an 8-digit message on your cell phone; please read it back to me," the agent said.

"1ZBT878X," I said.

"OK," replied the agent, "now look at your email and read the message I just sent you."

I opened the email and read it. ".45 caliber, 911 mode."

"Thank you," the agent said, "now we can talk."

Agent Jones informed me that the slug I sent the FBI lab had a very long history of homicides in the Keys. He spent the next thirty minutes recounting it.

The slug was first used in a homicide in Key Marathon in 2002 and pulled from the body of a Hispanic male teenager, approximately eighteen years old. The body was found stuffed under some mangrove trees along a bridge known as the Vaca Cut. The police investigated this homicide but had no suspects at the time. The next homicide occurred in 2006. The same bullet markings were found on the body of a Hispanic male about twenty years old who was a known drug dealer operating in the Lower Keys. The body was found in the Atlantic Ocean and was weighed down with several large rocks and a small boat anchor. The body had been eaten by crabs, fish, and sharks. There was no physical evidence found in the area. The police investigated this case and had no suspects. In 2007, another body was recovered in Key West with the same bullet markings. It had been thrown into the Atlantic Ocean and was identified as Juan Lopez, approximately twenty-five years old. The police investigation revealed several possible suspects; many were known drug dealers in the Keys, except one was a female named Maria

Gonzalez. The police located all these possible suspects, except Maria Gonzalez. Their investigation found the possible suspect called Maria Gonzalez did not exist.

"In 2016, the same bullet markings were found on the body of yet another Hispanic male, approximately eighteen years old. The body was found under some mangrove roots on Islamorada; like the others, it had been badly eaten away by crabs, fish, and other insects or animals. The body was identified as Jesus Altamirano. The police investigation revealed that the victim was involved with a younger juvenile whose nick name was Caliente. The police attempted to locate this juvenile but found no one with that name. This investigation, like the others, was still open. The latest homicide victim, Diego, was killed by the same bullet.

"Given the history of the homicides and the evidence that the same gun was used in all these cases, I hope you may have some substantial leads on this case," said Agent Jones. "If so, you should be able to solve five homicides that occurred in your area in the past nineteen years."

"You're telling me the bullet I sent you was fired from the same gun in five homicides occurring in the Keys over the past nineteen years?" I asked.

"Yes," Agent Jones replied. "In fact, this is one of the top ten homicides that we are actively seeking suspects for."

"How unusual is this type of evidence in your experience?" I asked.

"Like I told you, this one bullet marking was found in

five homicides over a nineteen-year period. It's very unusual. That's why I wanted to call you to alert you on the significance of your case," Agent Jones stated.

"Do you have any contact information from each of these homicides?" I asked.

"Yes," said Agent Jones.

"Can you send me copies of everything you have on this case?" I asked.

"Not sure I can send you everything yet; I need to clear it with my supervisor," he replied.

"OK," I replied, "how long will that process take?"

"Probably about one day, and given the history of these bullet markings, I anticipate your request will be no problem," Jones said. "As soon as I know, I will call you." He hung up.

Doaks came into my office and saw my expression. "What just hit you?" he asked.

"Well, sit down and listen to this," I said. I give Doaks a synopsis of what Agent Jones had said. Doaks's jaw hit the floor again.

"Dang, that is incredible," he said. "I've worked on several of these cases, and I did not know that bullet markings were a key piece of evidence. We need to let the sheriff know about this. Stay here, I'll contact his secretary to see if we can go and see him now." With that, Doaks left.

Two minutes later, he and the sheriff were at my office door. "Detective Hood," the sheriff said, "I understand you have some news on our latest homicide victim."

"Yes, sir," I replied, "please sit down and I will brief you on what I just learned from the FBI."

I spend the next twenty minutes detailing out the latest updates from the FBI, the latest fingerprint information, and the results of the videotapes from the bait shop.

"Will the FBI share their information on the bullet markings with you?" the sheriff asked.

"I am waiting on a call back from Agent Jones. He said he has to get his supervisor's approval," I told him.

"Pease keep me posted on this. As soon as you get that call, let me know." The sheriff got up, thanked me for my great work, and left.

"Well, rookie, welcome to the big time!" exclaimed Doaks.

What am I missing? I thought. I decided to call my botanist friend at the University of Miami. Dr. Phil Leaf answered the phone on the second ring.

"Katie?" he asked, "what's up?"

I told him about the homicide victim we found buried in the sand by the Hut. I explained to him that the medical examiner had found a piece of plant, leaf, or some type of plant material left in the plastic tarp covering the body.

"Can I send this piece of evidence to you for an analysis?" I asked.

"That depends," he said, "I am backed up for three weeks on similar requests from the Miami and Naples police departments,"

Crud, I thought. *I cannot wait three weeks.*

"Phil," I asked, "are these police departments investigating a murder case?"

"No," he replied.

"Well, I need to privately share something with you, and I would appreciate if you kept this information to yourself for the time being," I said.

"OK, what's going on?" he asked.

I told him about the two homicides I was investigating and the FBI reports. Then I told him we had a viable suspect but time was critical. I needed that analysis ASAP.

"Katie, this is huge!" he exclaimed. "In fact, this is one of the biggest cases I have ever heard of, let alone had the opportunity to work on."

After another few seconds, he said, "OK, I will do it ASAP, when can you get me this sample?"

"Can you hang on one minute?" I asked.

I looked around for Doaks. He came out of the men's room and saw me. "What now?" he asked.

"I need to do something unusual, and I need your advice," I told him.

"OK, what?"

I told him I needed to have an officer drive up to the University of Miami and give Dr. Leaf the evidence found in the plastic tarp covering Kennedy. He told me wait while he checked with the chief deputy. He left and came back in another minute and told me go ahead. I rushed back to my office and picked up the phone.

"Phil, I'll have one of our deputies drive up to your office and give you the evidence in the next few hours," I told him.

"Great, I will text you the quickest route up from the Keys to my office," he said. "I'll let you know my results in the next day or two." Then he hung up.

Ten minutes later, the deputy notified me that she was enroute to the university with the evidence. I texted her the driving instructions and told her to drive safely.

Doaks came into my office and sat down. "What's next, rookie?" he asked.

"How can I get these DNA samples to the private lab in Key West?" I asked.

"Not a problem, I know the lab director at the Key West facility, I'll call him and take the DNA evidence down today," he said.

*Is Doaks trying to be a nice superviso*r? I asked myself.

"Great," I said. "How long do you think it will take them to get some results for our investigation?"

"I already informed him about this case. I will tell him to rush it, and hopefully, we can get some results tomorrow," he said.

"Thanks," I said.

Doaks then informed me the financial detectives needed one more day to get enough probable cause to get a warrant to seize the Hut's financial records.

One more day, I thought, *what else can I be missing?* Doaks and I brainstormed for the next ten minutes. Nothing else seemed to jump out at us. Suddenly, my phone rang.

"Hello, Detective Hood speaking," I said.

The caller identified herself as Ronda. "Hello, Rhonda, how can I help you?" I asked.

"I have been hearing some rumors about a guy called Jack Kennedy, and I wanted to share some information I have on him," she said.

"Thank you for calling. What would you like to tell me?" I asked.

"I'm a member of the Hut on Point Key," Rhonda explained. "I saw Jack Kennedy lying on the beach here last week; I think on the 14th. I noticed that Maria was playing around with him on the beach. I then left and went back home. Later that day, I saw him walk up to my neighbor's house and go inside. I thought it was interesting, since that house belongs to Salsa, Maria's daughter. I also noticed that Mr. Kennedy spent the night and left after lunch the next day. I thought you might be interested in this information."

"Can I come down to your place to take a statement from you?" I asked.

"Sure, I would love to talk to you," she replied.

"Thanks, I will be there in fifteen minutes."

Doaks looked at me. "What was that about?" he asked.

I told him about Rhonda's phone call. As soon as I got up to leave, my phone rang again. "Hello, Detective Hood speaking," I said.

"Can I meet you at the Tiki Club at 5:00 p.m.?" the male caller asked.

"What is this regarding?" I asked.

"I saw someone dragging a body wrapped in plastic last week, and I saw that person bury the body along the seawall at the Hut," the caller said.

"Sure, I'll be there. How will you be dressed?" I asked.

Unfortunately, the caller had hung up.

"Doaks, how do you think I should handle this one?" I asked. Doaks got up and told me he'd be back in a second. He came back with the chief deputy, who I briefed on the updated information and the two phone calls. He told me he would assign three plainclothes deputies in the area ahead of the 5:00 p.m. meet time. Doaks gave me a thumbs up.

I left the department and headed to Rhonda's address. Doaks waved and headed to the private DNA lab. I arrive at Rhonda's address at 2:30 p.m. and exited my vehicle. As I was walking up the sidewalk, I heard yelling from the house next door. I rang the doorbell, and Rhonda met me. She invited me inside, but I told her to wait a second.

"Do you hear all that screaming and yelling?" I asked her.

"Yes, that happens every time Jairo, the wife's husband, returns from a long business trip," she replied.

"Is that Salsa's house you told me about earlier this day?" I asked.

"Yes, that is Salsa's house, and her husband Jairo just

arrived home."

"Do they have a screaming match every time he comes back from a trip?"

"Generally, but today there was a lot of extra screaming about a necklace, or something like that."

"A necklace?" I asked.

"Yes, I was doing my dishes when I heard Jairo accuse Salsa of sleeping with a man who left a necklace under their bed. After more yelling, Jairo started saying words in Spanish I didn't understand," she said.

"Rhonda, do you mind if I go over there to check things out?" I asked.

"No problem," Rhonda replied. I alerted dispatch that I was going into a residence on a welfare check for a possible domestic violence case. I also request a backup unit respond to my location ASAP.

I walked over to the house next door and knocked. Instantly, a man appeared.

"What do you want? Why are you here? Get out!" he yelled at me.

I identified myself as a detective with the Sheriff's Department, and he told me to f - -f and slammed the door!

Next, I heard more screaming and then slapping sounds. I entered the residence and found the man slapping the woman, who was lying on the floor. I told him to stop, and he charged me. I took him down and handcuffed him. After the arrest, two deputies came through the door, and took the man away in handcuffs. I went to check on the woman, who was pretty shaken up. By then, the medical techs had arrived. I contacted dispatch again and asked for a case number on this incident. Next, I asked the deputies to take the man to jail on domestic violence charges and to interrogate him if possible. Once the medical techs were done checking out the woman, I identified myself to her and asked if she could answer a few questions about this incident. During my interview, I learn a lot about her.

Her name was Salsa Rodriquez. She was a real estate broker in the Keys, married to Jairo for five years, had no children, and wanted to press charges against him. I ran a quick background check—DOB 8/1/1996, Hispanic female, five foot two, 105 pounds, brown eyes, and brown hair. She told me her husband was a very jealous man and believed she was having numerous affairs with a number of men in the area. She insisted that she was not and did not know how to convince him that she was loyal to him. I noticed a unique necklace lying on the floor behind the victim.

I pick it up. "What do you know about this necklace?" I asked her.

She immediately looked away. "Jairo told me he found this under our bed. I have never seen that before," she said.

"Can I take this?" I asked.

"Sure, I don't know where it came from, nor do I recognize it from any of my jewelry," she said. I took the necklace and put it into my pocket until I was able to get an evidence bag out of my car. I gave her a statement form and asked her to fill it out, which she did. I then asked her if she needed me to call anyone. She said no, she would be going over to her mother's apartment at the Hut in a few minutes. I gave her my card and asked her to call me if she needed any assistance from our department. I then left her house and returned to Rhonda's.

Rhonda was very excited and talkative. She wanted to know everything about what just happened next door. I calmed her down and told her the bare minimum of what had just happened. Then I began to interview her on her information. After fifteen minutes of talking, Rhonda gave me a statement. Her statement indicated that on August 16, a man similar in physical appearance to Jack Kennedy, who she had seen at the Hut earlier that day, arrived at Salsa's home around 6:30 p.m. He stayed the night and left her home around 1:30 p.m. the next day. He walked to her house, and when he left, he walked out and down the street.

I thanked her, handed her my business card, and asked her to give me a call if she had any additional information. I then put the necklace into an evidence bag and returned to my office.

I got to my desk and looked very closely at the necklace with the attached coin I had just put into evidence. The coin had some very unusual markings on it—a cross shape with a possible circle surrounding the cross—and the necklace chain looked like braided gold. I Google searched coin designs and after thirty minutes of looking, I found that this coin was taken off a treasure ship called the *Atocha*. The coin appeared to have a value of $3600. Google listed it as Mel Fisher's shipwreck treasure coin and stated that the coin was minted in Bolivia circa 1598–1621, had a denomination of 2 reale, with a Greek Cross on the front and the shield of King Phillip III of Spain on the back.

What the heck is this? I wondered. A treasure coin, a ship called the Atocha, and a mysterious necklace.

Doaks arrived five minutes later and told me that the DNA samples were delivered, and we would see some results tomorrow, with any luck.

I looked at my watch, 4:30 p.m. *Crud. Time to leave to meet this mystery person from the phone at the Tiki Hut.* I took the necklace down to property, checked it in, and told the property officer I'd be back in an hour to see it again. Then I left for the Tiki Hut.

At 4:45 p.m., I was sitting at the bar in the Tiki Hut and sipping a Coke when I noticed an older white male dressed in a work uniform enter the area and look over all the people here. He began to walk in my general direction but stopped when he noticed two other women sitting along the ocean view.

He hesitated and then walked toward me, sat down, and asked me if we could talk outside. I said yes, and both left the bar and headed to the parking lot. Three plainclothes officers followed us discreetly to the parking lot. I noted that they were close enough to help if needed but far away enough to give us our privacy. I turned to the man.

"Did you call me earlier today?" I asked.

"Yes, I did, but I needed you to come here, not stay in the restaurant," he said.

"Why?" I asked.

"I noticed two women from the social club at the Hut having an early dinner there. They are rumor creators and love to spread gossip about the members of the Hut and their affairs with other people," he told me.

"OK," I told him, "Who are you, and what type of information do you have for me?"

The man was extremely nervous. His eyes darted all over the place, and he kept rubbing his hands.

"Why are you so nervous?" I asked.

"Listen, detective, you don't know who you are dealing with in your investigation," he whispered.

"My name is Sam Decree. I work at the Hut as a maintenance man. I've worked there for eleven years, and I see and hear a lot about Maria Hernandez. I've heard that Maria has killed a lot of people over the past decade or so and that she has had numerous affairs with a lot of men involved in the drug business or treasure hunting. I'm afraid that she'll find out I'm talking to you, and she will kill me. But I wanted to tell you that on August 18, very early in the morning, I was working late on a pool pump under the sidewalk at the Hut. I was just about to leave the pump room when I heard this scraping sound. It sounded like someone dragging a heavy object over the concrete area. I waited until it was quiet and then peeked out the floor door. I saw Maria dragging something over to the seawall area, and then I saw her begin to dig into the sand. I waited about fifteen more minutes. I heard her say '*adios* a- - e.' I continued to watch and saw her kick the object into a shallow hole. Then I heard more shoveling. I stayed in the pump room another thirty minutes after she left. I wanted to make sure there was no one in the area. Then I immediately left and went home."

"Mr. Decree," I asked, "are you sure you saw Maria Hernandez do these things?"

"Yes," he said. "Maria and I have been friends and occasional lovers over the past eleven years. I know Maria Hernandez intimately, and I know it was her dragging the object and then burying it by the seawall."

"Will you come over to my office and give me a statement on what you just described?" I asked him?

"No, I can't," he replied.

"Why?"

"Two years ago, I heard Maria and her drug dealer Diego having a private conversation in the bar after the Hut was closed. Maria told Diego if he messed with her or her daughter, she would kill him, bury his body in the mangrove tress, and let the crabs eat him. She then showed him a gun. I am not sure what type of gun it was, but it was a gun. She smacked him with it on the jaw. Diego was stunned and made a move to hit her, but Maria put the gun in his groin and told him, 'Do it and you'll lose your manhood!' I cannot make any kind of statement to you. She'll kill me if she finds out. She has people everywhere."

"What if I were to provide you with protection from Maria and her people?" I asked him.

"How would you do that?" he asked.

"Let me call you in one hour. I need to check with my supervisor about this," I said.

"No," Sam insisted. "Too risky. I have seen what Maria can do when she is mad. I have heard her say she has killed three or four other people to protect her family. She somehow always knows a lot of information on these people, it's like she has some inside contact with a police agency. I know this because, I saw her and another man, supposedly a drug dealer in the area, having a heated argument one day. The man left, and Maria went into her office and called someone. Two minutes later, she had the man's name, address, and date of birth."

"Really? You observed all this? Where were you during the argument?" I asked him.

"I was fixing the toilet near the bar. I was lying on the floor, so no one knew I was there. I was going to defend her if needed, but when I heard the slap and saw the gun, I stayed put and waited until they left the bar. Then I walked by her office, and that's when I heard her ask someone for information on a license plate. So I can't give you anything at all unless you can guarantee me protection."

"OK, I understand, given the history of your information on Maria," I told him. "But if I can give you protection, would you be willing to give me a detailed statement on these incidents you've observed over the past two years?"

"Only, and only, if I can get a safe place to live, a new identity, and a new career somewhere off these Keys," Sam said.

"OK, please give me your cell phone number and I'll call you in an hour," I said. Sam looked around again and then scribbled his cell number down. He then walked away. He did not get into a car.

Crud, crud, crud, I thought, *how am I going to get protective custody on this guy?* I waved the three other officers off and returned to my car. I called Doaks and asked him to meet me at the station ASAP. I then made some notes on my phone on the information Decree had given me. I highlight several things: the gun, the murders of several people over the past decade or longer, some inside contact possibly involving the police, his eyewitness of the victim being buried by the seawall, numerous affairs, and treasure hunting.

All these things appeared to be vital information in closing this homicide case and perhaps five others.

Doaks called me up. "Rookie, let's meet at Rosa's. I am starving, and they have a chicken dinner special tonight. Can you be there in fifteen minutes?"

Dang Doaks, I thought, *I will need a raise just to keep*

you fed.

"OK, see you in fifteen minutes," I said.

I entered Rosa's and found Doaks at a booth, drinking coffee. "Hey," I said, sitting down.

"Rookie, what's going on?" he asked. "You look awful. What have you gotten yourself into now?"

The waitress came and took our order. I filled him in on the past three hours. Dinner came, we ate, and I continued to tell him about Sam Decree's information and the need for protective custody.

Doaks downed one more cup of coffee, looked at me, and said, "Hood, this is serious stuff. I've never asked the sheriff for protective custody for anyone in my thirty years here. I don't know how to do that."

"Look, there is a lot of potential evidence riding on this case," I said, "and given the links to five other homicides, I think we need to lay it all out in front of the sheriff."

Doaks agreed and exited the restaurant, leaving me the check. We met at the office, and although it was late, Doaks found the sheriff in his office and asked him if we could give him an update on this homicide case. The sheriff agreed, and we sat down at his conference table. Over the next hour, I went over everything I had investigated, heard, and found, and then I asked him about protective custody for Decree. The sheriff then looked at me and then at Doaks.

"I need to contact our county attorney about all of this," he finally said. "Can you brief him now if I can get him into my office?"

"Yes sir," I replied. The sheriff made a call. Fifteen minutes later, Mr. Don Moceri walked into the office. We all introduced ourselves and sat down. Over the next two hours, we briefed Moceri about our homicide investigation. He listened intently, took a lot of notes, then after we were done, asked both of us a lot of questions. Another hour passed, and Moceri informed the sheriff that we could go ahead and give Sam Decree a confidential informant status with full immunity and full protection until we can make a successful case against Maria Hernandez and her family.

Moceri then left, and the sheriff ordered us to start the protective process.

Chapter Eleven: Protection

August 23, 2021

Crud, crud, crud, I thought. *Decree will be going nuts now. I told him one hour, and now it's five hours later. Dang, I hope he's up.*

I dialed Decree's cell phone number. One, two, three rings. Finally, a sleepy sounding Sam answered.

"Hello," he said, "this better be important because I was just about to…"

A woman's voice cut him off in the background. "Sam, come here, I need you…"

I could tell he was about to hang up.

"Sam Decree, this is Detective Hood," I told him, trying to keep him on the line. "I got protective custody for you. Please wrap up your business there and let's meet."

"OK, OK, can you wait one minute? I need to tell Susan

something," he said.

Five minutes later, I was still listening to the interesting conversation between Decree and that Susan woman.

Finally, I heard a door slam. Then Decree was back on the phone. "OK, what do I need to do now?" he asked.

I gave Decree the address of a safe house located on the North Bay area of Marathon. I told him to pack enough clothes for a month and to get there as soon as possible. I hung up and went to my apartment to get some clothes for the next week. I then headed to the safe house.

Doaks arrived at the same time as me. "Wow," he said, looking at the safe house.

He headed into the house and turned on a light. I followed behind and looked around.

"This is a nice place," I told Doaks. "Who owns this?"

"I don't know, and I don't care. This place is great! Lots of room and a fully stocked refrigerator," Doaks said, heading down the hallway to claim a bedroom. I found another bedroom and threw my duffle bag on the bed.

Dang, it's going to be an interesting few days, I thought.

Sam Decree arrived ten minutes later. He came inside and looked around. "Nice place. Is this where I am staying?"

"Yes, you'll be staying here for a while," I replied. I told him to find a bedroom and then join us at the kitchen table. We needed to discuss some rules of protective custody.

An hour later, we were almost ready to go to bed. Decree did not like the fact he could not call anyone at any time. I explain to him that he wasn't allowed to use his cell phone until we figured out who was giving Maria all the confidential information.

Next, I told Decree to write a letter resigning from his position at the Hut, effective today. I directed him to have his final paycheck sent to a post office box in Key West.

I looked at the clock. It was 12:30 a.m. I told Decree and Doaks to go to bed. I then asked Decree for his car keys. He handed them to me shuffled down to his bedroom. I told Doaks I was going to go put Decree's car in the garage. I then moved my car into a parking lot away from our location. I headed back into the house.

At 1:00 a.m., I contacted dispatch and asked them to open an attached report on the domestic violence arrest I made earlier today. They received it and forwarded it to records. It was time for bed.

I woke up at 5:00 a.m. with a headache and a question floating around in my brain: *What am I missing?* I got up, turned on my laptop, and began listing all the leads we had discovered in the past twenty-four hours. I remembered that necklace, the treasure hunter statement by Decree, and the *Atocha* shipwreck. How were all these things connected?

I decided to Google the *Atocha* shipwreck. "Holy crap," I muttered. This shipwreck was worth a lot of money. I continued to scan the numerous articles about this shipwreck and found a photograph, which seemed to be about twenty years old. It showed the crew on the salvage ship that found the *Atocha*. There in the picture was a young Jack Kennedy.

Bingo, I thought. *This may be the connection I need to connect Maria Hernandez and Jack Kennedy.* I then Googled Jack Kennedy's name. There were too many Jack Kennedys in this database. I limited my search and found Jack Kennedy, our victim. The Google search results showed a picture of Jack on a pamphlet advertising charter boat fishing and sunken ship diving in the Bermuda area. He looked to be wearing the same coin and necklace I had just placed into evidence.

Interesting, I thought, *we may have just put together several pieces of information involving Salsa and her mother.*

I still needed to get a detailed statement from Decree in the morning. I hoped his testimony would be enough to get a search warrant for Maria Hernandez's residences. A critical piece of information still missing was finding out who Maria contacted to find out confidential information so quickly. I made a note to call the sheriff later. Two more critical things missing were the DNA results and the plant report from Dr. Leaf.

I closed my laptop and lay down for one minute. Then I heard Doaks slamming doors and water running.

I turned over and looked at my clock. 6:30 a.m. *Crud*.

I got up and headed to the kitchen. "Hood," Doaks yelled at me, "where is the coffee and the coffee pot?"

By 7:30 a.m., the coffee pot was going and Doaks and I had some. I went to check on Decree, who was still asleep. I looked at Doaks and told him we had a lot to do today. I needed to contact the sheriff about starting an Internal Affairs investigation to identify who was leaking confidential information to Maria Hernandez. Doaks said we need to get a court reporter here to take a detailed statement from Decree.

"Now, who should interview Decree? Me or you?" I asked Doaks.

"Both of us need to interview Decree. We need to cover everything he told you, and we need to get specific information to support a search warrant," he replied.

I agreed. Then my cell phone rang. It was Dr. Leaf. "Katie?"

"Yes, tell me."

"I wanted to inform you of my initial results. The plant leaf you sent me is not a leaf, it's the skin of an apple from the Manchineel Tree. They are called the little apples of death; in Spanish, they're called *la manzanitas de la muerte*. This plant can be deadly if administered right. Remember the Spanish explorer Ponce de Leon? He was poisoned by these apples when the native Indians shot at his soldiers looking for the fountain of youth. Leon was hit with an arrow that was dipped in the apple's residue. He died from the wound. The evidence sample is the skin off one of these apples. It can be deadly."

"You're kidding me!" I exclaimed. "Deadly?"

"Yes," Phil said. "If you do some research on this tree, which grows naturally in your area, you will find that it is deadly."

"Crud, crud, and more crud," I whispered. "Phil, in your opinion, how could you kill someone using this tree?"

"Interesting question, Katie. I would begin by peeling the skin off a number of these apples and then somehow put them into a wound on a body. I would also make a drink using the leaves and the skins from these little apples and have my victim drink this concoction. That would be a double whammy; it would probably kill the person," Phil replied.

"How does this poison work?" I asked.

"The poison works by cutting off the air supply, causing the throat to swell shut, and then the nervous system begins to shut down. It is a very painful, slow, suffocating death," Phil replied.

"Phil, I have one more thing I need you to do," I said. "Can you talk to Dr. Spock, our medical examiner, about your findings?"

"Sure, but why him?"

"Dr. Spock believes our victim, Jack Kennedy, was poisoned but he needs your advice on how to prove it. I think if you talk to him, he may find the evidence he needs to prove this victim was poisoned using this tree."

"Sure, just give him my number, and let's hope we can solve this homicide," Phil stated.

"Thanks. Please let me know when the evidence is ready to be returned and when your report can be submitted."

"OK." He hung up.

Doaks was listening intently to my half of the phone

conversation. He looked at me in astonishment. "Are you serious? This guy was poisoned by a tree growing in our area? How in the world does that happen?"

Decree entered the kitchen. "Where is the coffee?" he asked.

I poured him a cup and we sat down to discuss the day.

Two seconds later, a ton of bullets flew into the house from three sides. We were under attack. Doaks, Decree, and I hit the floor. I quickly dialed 911 on my cell.

"This is Detective Katie Hood. I urgently need back up at 202 South Palm Street. This is a safe house and we are under attack!" I told the dispatcher.

"Please stay on the line, and I will advise you when help is on the way," she told me.

"Listen, we are getting shot at here! Get the sheriff's department rolling their units here now and get off this line!" I hung up the phone.

Doaks ran toward his bedroom to get his gun. I had mine on me and began to creep over to the window on the east side of the house. There I saw two men armed with MP5 machine guns coming toward the front porch. I waited five seconds and then opened the door and shot both of them. Doaks headed to the west side of the house. He looked out the window and saw two other men armed with AK-47 rifles. He watched them climb up the back steps, waited about three seconds, and then opened the door and shot them.

Decree, meanwhile, had voided himself under the kitchen

table. "I don't want to die! I don't want to die!" he yelled at the top of his lungs.

"Shut up," I told him. "We are OK now, just hang in there. The calvary is coming."

Doaks and I returned to our positions. We look out the windows and saw a car leaving the area.

"Did you note the license plate or anything about that car?" I asked Doaks.

"No, nothing," he said.

Seconds later, five deputies arrived at our location. All had rifles at the ready position and were closely looking around. Doaks opened the door, flashed his badge and told them we were OK.

"Did you see any bodies in the area?" he asked the deputies. They said no.

Crud, crud, and crud, I thought. *How in the world did these guys know our location, and where are the four shot bodies?*

Sgt. Meade ran up the steps and asked if we were OK. Doaks and I told him we were fine but that there should be four bodies on the front and back steps. Meade directed his men to look at both locations. There were no bodies, but a lot of blood on the steps. I told Meade to secure the locations and have his deputies swab the areas for blood evidence. I then told Meade's other officers come into the house to help us locate bullets left in the walls, floors, and ceiling.

I felt my head spin. *Aren't we in a safe house with protective custody status? Why are we under attack? Who knows about this house*? These questions and my adrenaline dump sent my body into shivers.

I got to my bedroom, pulled on my sweatshirt, and went to find Decree. He was still under the table, shaking uncontrollably. "I am going to die! I knew she would find me! I knew she would try to kill me!" he continued to yell.

"Decree, shut up. Look around, you are OK. Please shut up, and let's get you cleaned up," I told him.

Ten minutes later, Doaks, Decree, and I are about to leave the safe house when the sheriff arrived on scene. He entered our kitchen, looked around, and saw the bullet holes in the walls, floor, and ceiling. "Are you all right, anyone hit?" he asked.

"No one hit, only damage is the house," Doaks told him.

"Good, we are moving you out now," he said. "Please go to this address now. I will have three patrol units at that location to check for any surveillance devices or anything else unusual." He then called Doaks over to the hallway and whispered something. Doaks listened very intently. Then the Sheriff left and we packed up our belongings and got out the front door.

Doaks grabbed my arm as we were going down the steps.

"Listen," he said, "follow me very closely as we leave this area and stay on my bumper. We are *not* going to this location, that's just a ploy to get the bad guys to show up. Just stay on my bumper." He then got into his car and left.

Decree and I got into my patrol car. I ordered one of the

deputies still in the area to take Decree's car and put it into our police compound. We left. Two minutes later, Doaks made a U-turn and headed down Route One toward the Seven Mile Bridge. I followed him. Just before we reached the bridge, Doaks made another U-turn and headed south onto a roadway covered with grass and palm fronds. Within seconds, our cars were hidden by the brush bushes and undergrowth on this road. We continued on this road until we ended up in a clearing. Doaks then turned left at a large tree and stopped his vehicle. I watched as Doaks left his car and entered a large camouflage tent.

Dang, I thought, *I didn't see that coming*! In fact, I hadn't recognized the structure at all, let alone it being a tent! I told Decree to get out of the car and follow me.

"Wow." Decree said. "This is just like another home, only it's a tent."

Doaks left the tent and came back fifteen minutes later.

"Where did you go?" I asked him.

"I went to camouflage the cars," he replied. "Let's get settled in and discuss what our next steps in this investigation are."

Two minutes after we had just poured coffee, Doaks's cell phone rang. It was the sheriff.

"Yes, Sheriff," he answered.

"Listen very carefully to your next instructions. First, take all your cell phones and put them into a safe in the green bedroom. The safe is coated to prevent any type of tracing device. Next, in the stove under the broiler, there are two cell phones. Take them out. In the empty cream carton in refrigerator, there are charging units for these phones. Charge the phones and only use them to contact me at this number. I want you to walk into the closet in the hallway. Open the door, pull the jackets away from the back wall, and then pull on the light string. There should be a false wall moving once you pull that string. Look inside the room. There are a number of weapons for you and Hood to use if you need to protect your witness. Also, this safe room has a tunnel that leads to Boat Harbor Landing. If you need to use this, you'll see a green older-looking speedboat tied to the dock. Under the passenger seat are the boat keys to use to leave the area. You need to know that we have a lead on an individual working in our department who may be involved in this morning's attack. I'll keep you updated as our internal affairs investigation progresses on this individual. Now, do you have any questions?"

"Yes, sir, if we have some additional information on this homicide case," Doaks said. "How can we update you?"

"You can contact me at this number, and only this number, when you have additional information or when you need me to coordinate any follow-up investigations," he replied.

"No other questions, sir," Doaks said and then disconnected his cell. He headed toward the bathroom. "Hood, please put your cell phone and Sam's on the table. I'll be right back."

Doaks came back and told Decree and I what the sheriff had directed him to do.

"Crap, I don't get a cell phone. Why? Decree whined.

"Listen, Decree, you need to understand very clearly what the heck is going on here. I don't want you or me or Doaks to be killed. So just take a chill pill, and drink your coffee," I ordered him.

After we'd followed all the orders from the sheriff, we all sat at the kitchen table and began to talk. During the next hour, we all agreed on these facts: Maria Hernandez was probably the one person who arranged this morning's attack on our safe house. We also suspected she had a mole inside our department. The mole gave her this classified safe house information and had access to a lot more information on our homicide case. We also speculated that Maria operated a large criminal business in our area, if not all the Keys. We needed to find out how large her organization was and how we could expose it.

Decree began to yawn and told us he was going to the couch to take a nap. Doaks told him not to touch our cell phones. Doaks and I then begin to review all the information we now had on our homicide cases. I wrote a list of things we knew and another list of things we needed to prove. I start with the list of things we knew:

"We have four bodies; one is Jack, the other is a Diego, plus two unknowns. We have fingerprints of Jack and Maria on the bait box container located at Diego's homicide scene. We have the bullet taken out of Diego's body. We have five other homicides connected to this gun with these bullet ballistics. We have Jack Kennedy connected to a lot of related criminal cases including murder, embezzlement, and kidnapping. We have security camera footage of Maria buying three boxes of bait from Captain Hooks the morning that Diego was killed. We believe that Jack was poisoned, probably by Maria, but we don't know why. We know there are several ongoing financial investigations involving Maria with the state and federal governments.

"Now, the list of things we need to prove: to begin, we need to interrogate Sam Decree. His statement could link Maria to Jack's burial and perhaps to the scene of Jack's murder. We need to get a detailed description of the gun Sam saw Maria threaten one of her drug dealers with. We need to tie Maria to these five other homicides. We need the results of the DNA on the two babies' bodies. We need to tie the coin necklace I found in Salsa's house to Jack Kennedy and find out why this necklace was at Salsa's. We need to identify the blood evidence left at the safe house this morning. We need to use any of the information the DPS and the IRS have on Maria Hernandez's finances involving the Hut and any other property."

Just then, the cell phone rang. Doaks answered it.

"Hello," he said.

"Doaks, this is the sheriff. I wanted to give you some more information on our internal affairs investigation on the mole in our department. We identified the mole as Dispatch Supervisor James Jose. He is Maria's first cousin. We checked his office phone and his cell phone and found numerous calls between him and Maria over the past years. In fact, he was the one who phoned Maria about the safe house, and we believe she organized the attack this morning. We went to James's house; he was dead. It looks like an apparent suicide. We found a lengthy confession apparently left by James detailing his work with Maria. Unfortunately, we believe he may have given her your new location, so we want you to move now. Please leave the tent and go to your cars."

Just as we were about to leave, there was a huge explosion outside. It knocked us to the ground.

"What was that? Are you all OK?" the sheriff asked over the phone.

"I think our cars just exploded," Doaks said. "We need to leave using the safe room now!"

The sheriff agreed and hung up. Doaks and I took Decree and ran toward the safe room. As soon as we entered the room, the south side of the tent blew up. We closed the safe room's door and headed down the tunnel. Using the head lamps on our helmets, we followed the tunnel and came out in a garage adjacent to the Reef Restaurant in Boat Harbor. We ran over to the green speedboat, I threw Doaks the keys, and we left the area. As we were heading north along the shoreline, I called the sheriff.

"Sheriff, Hood here," I told him.

"Hood, what happened?" he asked.

"Our location was compromised again. We heard two explosions. We knew we were being attacked again when the south side of our tent blew up. We left the area using the safe room tunnel, and now we are in the boat heading north along the shoreline of Marathon."

"Keep heading north. I will have a Coast Guard Cutter meet—"

He was cut off by a loud explosion on his end.

"Sheriff, Sheriff, are you OK?" I yelled into the phone. I waited and listened; I heard the Sheriff barking orders to everyone in the area. I heard him yelling at them to check the compound and the surrounding area for casualties and get the medics here ASAP!

"Hood, I'm OK, I need to go. Follow your current route north. In fifteen minutes, you'll see a large Coast Guard Cutter in the cut between Marathon and Duck Key. Rendezvous there on the south side of Duck Key."

He hung up the phone, and I gave Doaks our new rendezvous location. There about one quarter mile away, on our left side, was the biggest boat I'd ever seen in this area.

"It's the Coast Guard Cutter!" I yelled at Doaks. "Perhaps we will be safe on that thing."

"Let's hope," he yelled back at me as we headed toward the Cutter. We came along the east side of the ship and were greeted by four fully armed men who immediately asked for our police identification. Both Doaks and I flashed our badges to the men, who then took possession of our boat. We climbed up a contraception that looked like a gang plank device and arrived on the main deck. A man dressed in full battle gear with a lot of bars on his shoulders and symbols on his helmet approached us.

"Detectives Doaks and Hood and Mr. Decree?" he asked.

"Yes." We all nodded.

"Good. I'm Captain Nimoy; please come with me," he said. We all followed him into the ship's galley.

Chapter Twelve: Warrants

August 24, 2021

We arrived in the galley of the huge ship. Captain Nimoy asked if anyone was injured. We all said no and asked if we could we have a cup of coffee. Within seconds, four steaming hot coffee mugs appeared. The captain informed us that we were going to be onboard his ship for a while. Due to the continuous attacks on the safe houses, the sheriff had asked permission for all of us to stay onboard until search warrants were executed at Maria Hernandez's Hut and private residences sometime in the next forty-eight hours.

Doaks looked at me. "Hood, what are your feelings about that?"

"I had hoped to be involved in the searching of the Hut and Hernandez's private residences," I replied.

"That's not going to happen," the captain interjected.

DR. H

"We are thirty miles into the Gulf of Mexico and will not rendezvous with the Sheriff's boat until next Monday."

Crud, crud, and more crud, I really wanted to be there when these search warrants were executed, I thought. I could see Doaks was upset too, but then I had an idea.

"Captain, do you have a legal stenographer on board?" I asked.

"Yes, we do," he replied. "Ms. Wright is onboard taking a number of statements from various crew members. We were involved in a tragic accident last month in which two of our sailors were killed during a battle drill. The Coast Guard is required to have a formal inquiry following the death of any on board personnel during a planned exercise," he stated.

My mind started racing. I looked at Doaks. "Doaks, could we use this stenographer to take Decree's statement?"

"Do you have a phone that I can use to call our district attorney?" Doaks asked the captain.

"Sure, come with me, and I will arrange it," he said. They took off to another part of the ship.

Decree then looked at me. "I think I am getting seasick." Then he barfed all over the floor."

Great, I thought. *Well, I guess it could be worse; we are alive despite being involved in two attacks"*

Decree ended up at a big sink, and I could hear him vomiting more. I left the area to find someone to help me clean up his mess.

Twenty minutes later, Doaks returned to the galley.

"Where is Decree? he asked.

"He is seasick and is lying down in one of the officer quarters we're going to be staying in," I told him. "What did Morceri tell you about using this federal stenographer to take Decree's statement?"

"He wants to be here during our interview to make sure we cover all the crimes Decree has heard of or seen over the past few months or years," Doaks said.

"Great, when is he coming?"

"Two days. He wants to be there during the search warrants service at the Hut and at Hernandez's residences," Doaks stated.

Me too, I thought, *but here we are in the middle of the Gulf of Mexico so that's not going to happen!*

I then looked at Doaks and told him an idea. "Doaks, given the amount of time we have prior to Moceri getting on board, let's brainstorm areas where we can use Decree's information to develop enough probable cause to arrest Maria Hernandez."

"Great idea, rookie. You go ahead and get the big areas mapped out. I am going to take a shower and then a nap. This has been a long day, and it's only 1:00 p.m." Doaks then left the galley to find his new bedroom suite on the ship.

I settled into a large booth and pulled out my laptop. I started to list some things. Before long, I lay my head down.

"Miss, miss, miss. Please wake up, we need to start our dinner preparations," the sailor said, shaking me.

DR. H

"Oops, I am so sorry. I will get out of your way now," I said and left the galley. I looked at my watch—*crud, I was asleep for three hours. Now, where is my room on this ship?* I found one of the sailors with lots of ribbons on his shoulders and tapped his arm.

"Excuse me, sir, could you direct me to my room?"

"Yes, ma'am, please follow me," he said and took off down another hallway. He stopped at room door six. "This is your room."

"Thanks," I said and opened my door. The room was tiny. There was a bed, or what looked like a bed, on a metal thing attached to the wall. I looked at a toilet combined with a shower head. *How will this work?* I wondered. I looked for a place to hang up my clothes. Well, I only had one pair of pants, one shirt, two boots, socks, and underwear.

This is not going to cut it, I thought.

I opened the door and there was Doaks. "Nice room," he chuckled, looking in. "How do you like the bathroom facilities? You can go to the bathroom while showering!"

"Shut up, Doaks. We need more clothes; mine are soaked."

Just then, the captain arrived with a bundle of women's clothing.

He asked if I was a size five or four. I told him four, and he handed me a complete package of clothing, including underwear, socks, shoes, and an interesting one-piece uniform. On the breast pocket in big letters were the words *civilian personnel.*

He then turned to Doaks. "Let's go, I'll get you outfitted in the Quartermaster's room." Doaks waved goodbye and followed the captain. I closed and lock the door, took off my wet clothes, and had a long, hot shower. I put on all the dry clothes, and to my relief, every piece fit me perfectly. *Great*, I told myself, *now I just need one more cup of coffee.* I headed out to the galley.

As I was walking to the galley, the captain called me over. "Detective Hood," he said.

"Yes, sir, "I responded.

"I want to inform you and Sgt. Doaks that your boat was wired to explode about twenty minutes after you left Boat Harbor. Your sheriff contacted me and requested that the boat be immediately inspected for any bombs or devices. Our bomb technicians found a large time bomb connected to the fuel line. The device was defused and destroyed. You may want to thank your sheriff once we are done with our mission," he said.

"Yes, sir, and please tell your men thank you for saving our lives and that of countless others on your ship," I said.

One hour later, I had eaten some delicious food and had two cups of coffee. I went back to my room and turned on my laptop. Thankfully, I had put it in my waterproof backpack during our escapes.

I looked around for Doaks and found him coming out of the restroom by the galley.

"Doaks, let's go to the galley and talk," I said.

"OK, Rookie, what are we talking about?"

"Captain informed me that his bomb technicians inspected our boat and found a time bomb strapped to the fuel line. They defused and destroyed the device. I think you needed to know that, and I think we need to call the Sheriff and tell him thanks," I told him.

"Holy crap!" Doaks yelled. "You have got to be kidding me."

"No joke, Doaks, we are very, very lucky that the boat didn't blow up when we left Boat Harbor," I stated.

Doaks looked at the sky above. I think he said a silent prayer thanking the Good Lord for saving us once again.

"Now," I told him, "Let's get to work on the interview questions. I want to get all the main points we need to go over with Decree identified. Then I need to outline our interview questions to make sure all these points are covered."

Doaks nodded and we went to the galley.

We saw Decree in the galley. He wasn't green anymore but was walking at a slant and wasn't looking good. I went over to him. "Are you feeling, OK?"

"No, I am still very dizzy, and my stomach is killing me," he said.

"Did you ask one of the sailors to get you to the sick bay on the ship?" I asked.

"No, I'm just happy to be standing and not puking my guts out again," he said. I grabbed his arm and found another sailor with some stripes on his shoulder.

"Can you please take Mr. Decree to the sick bay?" I asked him. "He is seasick and needs a doctor." The sailor took Decree and headed to another part of the ship.

In the meantime, Doaks found us a secluded table and had two steaming cups of coffee waiting. "Thanks," I told him. "Now, let's get started."

Over the next two hours, Doaks and I outlined everything we could remember from our numerous conversations with Decree. We identified these as our main talking points: starting on August 17, what did he see and hear from his position in the pump room? How did he know it was Maria and not someone else moving the body? Did he remember exactly what time and date he observed these things? Could he remember the date and time when he heard the conversation between Maria and this drug dealer? Exactly what did he see and hear? Did he see the gun Maria was pointing at or waving at the drug dealer Diego? If so, could he describe it? Could he describe Diego's, height, weight, appearance, jewelry, or anything else? Did he remember the time of day and the date he heard this conversation? What did he observe when Maria was making those phone calls to someone in the police department? What did he remember about Maria's statements on killing lots of people? Could he remember the time of day or the day of week he heard these statements? Could he describe his relationship with Maria Hernandez over the past decade?

"Now, what are we missing?" I asked Doaks.

Doaks took a long sip of his coffee and then looked around the room. "I'm worried about his relationship with Maria Hernandez," he said.

"OK, why?" I asked.

"Because if he and Maria were lovers and their relationship has continued on and off over the past decade, I am not sure how the district attorney will react to anything Decree has told us."

"What if we can demonstrate to Mr. Moceri that Maria sleeps around and has had a number of affairs with a lot of men over this same time period? Would that impact Decree's truthfulness?"

"Good question, rookie. I don't know," Doaks said. Then he looked at the clock in the galley. "I am going to bed."

Great, I told myself again, *here I am, still thinking about all the areas we need to cover in this one-shot interview. What am I still missing?* I headed down toward my room when I something struck me. Where had I put our new cellphones? I looked around for another sailor person. I had almost reached my room when the captain appeared in the hallway.

"Captain, I want to thank you for all you and your crew are doing for us. I was wondering if you confiscated our cellphones once we came onboard." I asked.

"Yes, I took two phones and placed them in a drying bin and had them recharged. If you need your phone, follow me. I'll take you to our equipment locker."

Fifteen minutes later, I was in my bed with a fully charged cellphone. I fell asleep.

At 6:30 a.m. the next day, I heard lots of bells going off. *What are those sounds, where am I, and what is going on?* I wondered.

I got up and opened my door to see sailors running toward the outside decks. Then I heard gunfire. I looked outside on the main deck and saw two things: one was a boat leaving the area that appeared to be on fire and the other was that our Coast Guard ship seemed to be zig zagging. I was hanging on a rail when Doaks stumbled out of his room.

"What the h- -l is going on?" he asked.

I told him I didn't know but it seemed like we were under attack again. I pointed out to the sea on our left and watched a boat blow up.

Our ship quickly made a U-turn and headed toward what was left of that boat. Doaks and I watched as the Coast Guard commander sent an inflatable boat to the location. Within seconds, we saw there were no survivors.

The boat was completely destroyed. Doaks turned to me. "You don't think Maria Hernandez knew we were on this ship and sent these guys to attack the Coast Guard Cutter, do you?"

I looked at him and wondered how in the world she knew about the Coast Guard Cutter. "I would not put anything past this woman; she always seems to be one step ahead of us," I said.

During the next hour, the captain held a number of debriefing sessions with his crew. He asked Doaks and me to attend the officers' debriefing session taking place in ten minutes. We went to the officer's mess and were told what happened. The Captain told his command staff that around 6:00 a.m., the radar controller noticed a fast-approaching boat heading in our direction. The boat continued a course to ram the ship. The watch commander took evasive actions, and the Cutter was fired upon. The Cutter returned fire. As soon as the Cutter returned fire, the radar controller noticed that a torpedo was launched from the boat toward the ship. The watch commander initiated evasive actions, and the torpedo did not strike the ship. As the speedboat was leaving, it exploded. Our tactical response team launched our inflatable boat and located the scene where the boat exploded. There were no survivors. The Captain then said he had filed a report with the admiral, and we were to continue our mission in the Gulf until further notice.

Crud, crud, and crud, I thought. *How does this woman know everything about our protection program?* The captain waved us over to his table. He asked us to join him for coffee and a conversation.

We sat down. "Do you think there is a mole in your department?" the captain asked.

"Yes sir, we conducted an internal affairs investigation in our department to find the source of the leak," said Doaks. "The sheriff informed us last night that he had located the mole, but when the SWAT team went to his house to arrest him, they found he had committed suicide."

The captain then looked at me and Doaks one more time. "Do you think there may be another leak in your department?"

"I don't know sir, but with your permission, I would like us to call our sheriff on a secure line and discuss these recent events," Doaks said.

The captain agreed and he and Doaks left to call the sheriff. Crud, I was alone again.

Just then, Decree entered the galley. He looked awful. He saw me sitting at a table, grabbed a cup of coffee, and joined me.

"Hood, can you tell me what the heck were all those bells and the gunfire and the explosion this morning?" he asked.

"Decree, we were attacked this morning by another boat. The boat tried to sink us with a torpedo, but the attackers were blown up," I told him.

"Crap, I knew she would find us, and I knew she would not stop attacking us until I was killed," Decree sighed.

"Look, Decree, we are safe, and we aren't going to be attacked again," I assured him. "Maria will be in jail within the next twelve hours. Now you're safe, and you won't be harmed."

"How are you so sure Maria will be in jail in the next twelve hours?" he asked.

"In a few hours, the IRS and our DPS financial crimes

units will be serving search warrants at all of Maria's residences and at the Hut," I told him.

Decree then looked at me and turned a different shade of white.

"Decree, what's wrong?" I asked.

"Maria has three escape routes in her properties. She also has five different passports and a ton of money stashed in a go bag just in case the cops show up," he said. "She will get away, and then she will disappear. I know this because she showed me the passports and the money she has stashed in her penthouse."

Crud, I told myself. *I have to let the Sheriff know.*

"Can you remember anything else that Maria might do or might have stashed away to help her escape?" I asked him.

Decree said no but looked very nervous. He excused himself to go to the restroom.

Crud, crud, and more crud, I told myself, *what can I do to prevent her from escaping when the warrant teams hit her locations?* I thought for a second and then grabbed my cell phone to call the Sheriff. I was just about to dial his number when I remembered Doaks was on the phone with the Sheriff. Who could I contact? Two names came up—Moceri and Clutch.

I immediately dialed Moceri's personal cell number.

"Hello. Hood, what is it?" he asked.

"Moceri, you need to know that Maria has several escape routes in all her residences, and she has five passports and a ton of money in a go bag. I believe she will be out of her residences or the Hut minutes after your serve your warrants," I told him.

"Crap," Moceri said. "Can Decree give us any more specifics on her routes, the passports, or the money?"

"No," I told him. "He is very afraid, and he truly believes you will never catch Maria."

"If you were in my shoes, what plan of action would you take, given this information?" Moceri asked me.

I thought for a few moments. Then I said, "I would alert the Coast Guard Station in Marathon and ask them to put up two or three of their helicopters to circle all the residences owed my Maria Hernandez. In addition, I would put as many of the sheriff's patrol boats as possible in the Atlantic or in the Gulf to monitor any unusual activities once the warrants are served. I would also contact the admiral in charge of the Coast Guard operations in the Keys to see if there is an Airborne Warning and Control System (AWACS) aircraft in the air during the warrant service. The admiral can authorize this AWACS to an emergency listening operation over the Marathon Key to monitor any phone contacts made by Maria to her associates if she tries to get off the island."

"Great ideas," Moceri said. "I will be on it now." He hung up.

Next, I called Clutch. "Hood, what the heck do you need now?" he asked. I quickly told him what was going on and what I had suggested to Moceri.

"Wow," Clutch stated. "Great ideas. Can I suggest one

more? I have two remote drones located at the sheriff's department. I could get the drones in the air in about five minutes. Can you give me the addresses of the residences our DPS officers will be serving warrants on?"

I gave Clutch the addresses. He hung up, and I waited. My wait seemed to last hours, if not days.

Twenty minutes later, Doaks ran into the galley. "Hood, you will not believe this," he panted. "Maria Hernandez is related to our midnight patrol commander; he was the one giving her all the classified information on our protection program. He left the station last night around 1:00 a.m. and has since been reported missing. The Sheriff put out an APB (all-points bulletin) on him and his vehicle. I hope we can find that S.O.B soon. He has cost our department a lot of injuries. Thankfully, no one was killed."

Crud, I thought to myself, *can anyone be trusted in our department given the actions of Maria Hernandez recently?*

"Doaks, you need to know what Decree has told me and what I've passed onto Moceri," I told him. Over the next ten minutes, I filled him in on all the information.

"Wow," Doaks exclaimed, "that is incredible."

"Well, let's hope we hit the jackpot on our warrants and on her arrest," I told Doaks.

Then it was time for us to wait. The wait seemed to last another several hours; in reality, we waited about ten minutes before my cell phone rang.

"Hood, this is Moceri. I wanted to tell you that all the

aircraft, boats, and AWACS are in place. Your sheriff is coordinating everything and hopefully, we will have an arrest and some seized financial records soon," he stated. He then thanked me and hung up.

Ten minutes later, the captain appeared and asked Doaks and me to join him in the command tower. We left the galley and walked up a lot of steps, holding onto metal stairway until we reached the top of the ship where the command center was located. There, the captain directed us to a television monitor and told to watch the action about to occur.

"What are we watching?" I asked the captain.

"The deputy director of your DPS operations contacted me five minutes ago and has linked the video feeds from two drones flying over the Maria Hernandez's residences into our location. He said to please bring you up here to watch the fireworks!"

The captain looked at me and asked, "Who is this man?"

Just as I was about to tell him, the drones picked up a lot of noise, then explosions, then gunfire, and then nothing. The television screen went black. The technician in the command tower told the captain the drones must have been shot out of the air.

How can this be happening? I thought. Doaks and the captain were thinking the same thing. Just then, my phone rang.

"Hood," Clutch said, "I can't believe this. That woman shot down the drones and has initiated a war against our warrant teams and the aircraft in the area."

"Clutch, I believe she is capable of doing many things, but I'd suggest you alert the officers to watch the sea surrounding her residence. I believe she is using all of this to divert our attention from her escape route," I told him. He agreed and hung up the phone.

For the next fifteen minutes, the silence in the command tower was deafening. None of our phones rang. The captain did not receive any orders or instructions from the admiral at the command center in Miami. These moments are the worse part of a police officer's investigation. Tons of action going on at the warrant site, while we all sat in silence fifty miles away.

Chapter Thirteen: Autopsy

August 29, 2021

Dr. Spock's autopsy report was dated August 29, 2021. The body he examined on this date was confirmed to be that of Maria Gonzalez Hernandez. The cause of death was multiple gunshots and shrapnel wounds to her torso and head.

Maria Hernandez was dead. According to the numerous police reports made after the warrant service at the Hut and her residences, Maria decided to take on the cops and the IRS and the DPS officers in a large gun battle. Once the shooting started, she was seen running toward a hidden cave along the south side of the Atlantic Ocean when she blew up a dozen claymore mines, killing numerous officers. The Coast Guard Helicopters, fired at her, and she returned fire. She was killed in the firefight, and her body landed on a claymore mine that had a time delayed switch. As the officers were converging on her last known location, they observed a body flying in the air, immediately following an explosion of one more claymore mine. Dr. Spock's last entry on his autopsy reported indicated that Maria was pregnant at the time and that she had a small amount of cocaine in her system.

Doaks looked at me. "Crap, rookie, I wanted to have a closure on all these old homicides and criminal cases," he said.

"Well, I would have loved to clear up all these cases, but until we find some more evidence that proves Maria was involved, our case is closed," I said. "Hey, Doaks, when are you going to promote me from rookie to detective?"

"Not sure, rookie, but you did one great job on this case, and I expect you to continue in the same manner in future cases."

Doaks then left my office and headed toward the men's room.

Epilogue

September 13, 2021

Two weeks later, Dr. Spock contacted me and Doaks. On this conference call, he told us

that the body he had examined and confirmed to be Maria Hernandez was not her but the

body of her identical twin sister, Selena.

Coming Soon in January 2024…

The Hunt begins:
Where is Maria Hernandez? Where is the *Isabella*? How will Katie and Doaks solve the cold case homicides and link Maria Hernandez to the six or seven murder victims? Whose babies are buried in the sand by the Hut's seawall? Does the restaurant called the Hut still exist?

These questions and others will be solved in the next book titled:

The Hunt

You can follow Dr. H as the Hunt is written by going to his website: harryhueston.com.

Made in the USA
Columbia, SC
21 June 2022